Ink
Or
Swim

A Dakota Maddison Tattoo Shop Mystery
Book 1

First paperback edition June 2023

Book cover design by Nirkri@fiverr

Dakota Maddison logo by @sirbro_ink.az

ISBN 978-1-7367559-8-3 (paperback)
ISBN 978-1-7367559-9-0 (ebook)

www.trisharrowsmithauthor.com

For Be,
For their support and encouragement
through all my ups and downs, both with
writing and with life.

Chapter 1

Echoes of my own footsteps were all I could hear as I made my way down the hall. I took a deep breath and opened the door just wide enough so I could slip through. I was later than I intended to be, but it sounded like I made it to the town hall meeting just in time. I didn't worry much about it when I was in the city, but now that I lived in and owned a business in a small town, it was important to me to know what was happening around me.

Despite the chill still present in the evenings, I shivered from the icy blast of the air conditioning vent directly above me. The hoodie and jeans I had on were no match for the arctic setting the system had been set to. I have only been in town, officially, for two days and spent most of the time by myself, getting ready for my shop's opening. I hadn't taken the time to introduce myself to many people. Of those people I have met, several of them had already warned me about Annette. Rumor had it she was crass, the town gossip, and extremely averse to change. I could see exactly what people were saying about her now.

She was standing in the middle of the room, demanding attention. "All I'm saying is, we have two days left until this... shop... opens and we should be banding together to stop it before our town becomes overrun by hoodlums and motorcycle gangs. This is a peaceful area and we owe it to our residents and tourists to keep it crime free."

The heavy, wooden door behind me chose the most inopportune time to latch shut. Every attendee turned their head in my direction. I mumbled through gritted teeth. "Sorry."

Annette used my presence to her advantage even though the look on her face told me she was annoyed by the disruption. "Well, I don't know who you are but you're a perfect example." She turned toward the front of the room again. "See her? She's tiny. How is she supposed to protect herself from some biker?" She spat the last word out, conveying her disgust. "How are any of us supposed to defend ourselves against an entire gang?"

"They're clubs."

Seething from the second interruption, she spun around, crimson faced. "Excuse me?"

I stepped forward and raised my voice to ensure the entire room could hear me. "They're motorcycle clubs, not gangs."

Annette rolled her eyes to the ceiling. "You're arguing over my word choice? I'm... I'm sorry, but who are you? And why should I give a rat's tail what you think?"

I squared my shoulders and flashed a comically large smile. "I'm Dakota Maddison, owner of Satin Mystique Tattoo. I believe it's my friends you feel you need to protect everyone from."

She put her hand over her heart and gasped. "You?" Her mouth fell open for a moment. "You're the one who owns the tattoo shop? But you look so...normal."

I smirked and nodded, watching as she tried to sort it out in her head. I was never sure what people assumed tattoo artists were supposed to look like, but I did know it wasn't like me. I stood barely over five feet tall, had shoulder length blonde hair, and wore just enough makeup to accentuate my features. People often told me I looked 'too innocent' to be an artist because I didn't have any visible tattoos if my arms and legs were covered. "What am I supposed to look like?"

Annette sat down quietly, embarrassed by her words, and didn't speak again for the remainder of the evening. Night had moved in and I was thankful for the lights in the parking lot as I walked to my Jeep. Just as I reached it, I heard someone call out my name. I turned back to see a petite brunette walking briskly toward me.

"Hey. I just wanted to apologize for Annette. She's always quick to judge."

"That's okay, it's not your job to apologize for her. People can have their own opinion, even when that opinion is based on bias rather than fact." It was nice of her to apologize on behalf of Annette, but I learned a long time ago that many people are set in their ways; no matter what you do or say, or how many facts you present, you can't change their opinion.

"Well, she can come across harshly at times. But she's also not wrong. No one in this town wants you or your criminal friends here."

Her attitude changed so fast it made me wonder what her true motive was for coming to speak to me.

"Huh. That's so weird because between myself and my guest artists, we have over fifty residents signed up to come in for tattoos during our grand opening weekend. Makes me think maybe some people do want me here." I reached forward and opened my car door. "And my friends aren't criminals."

"I'm not done talking to you." She raised her voice loud enough that a small group of people stopped to watch. "I want to know why you're here."

My heart was beginning to race and I could feel the flush crawling across my cheeks. I had to remind myself to keep my temper at bay. "Why I'm here? I'm here because I want to be. I moved away from the city because I wanted a quieter life, a slower pace. My parents and I stayed here every year during the summers when I was growing up and I liked the town. Now, is that all or would you like to know what I had for breakfast as well?"

She rolled her eyes. "I just want to be clear. We don't want you here. I would recommend looking for another place to open your *little* shop before you embarrass yourself."

"I have no intention of doing either of those things, but I appreciate your concern." I got in my car and took a quick look around before slamming the door shut. It looked as though everyone from the meeting had formed a crowd around us. I wondered how many of those people felt the same way.

I woke up early the next morning, showered, and went to the coffee shop across the street from my tattoo shop. I prefer to make my first cup of coffee at home but having only been in town for two days, I'd focused my efforts on making sure the shop was ready to open.

My own house suffered the consequences of limited time and cardboard boxes still housed the majority of my belongings.

I thought I had planned far enough in advance but between closing my old shop and opening the new one, it seemed as if my to-do list continued to grow no matter how many items I crossed off. "Good morning. Caffe macchiato, please."

"Good morning."

I handed over my card. "You'll see me quite a bit. I'm Dakota. I'm opening the tattoo shop across the street."

"Oh, that's you?" Her red hair fell in long, wide curls around her face. Between her hair, height, and lips, she reminded me of Jessica Rabbit. "I didn't put a face to your name, but you have quite a reputation around here already."

"I do? Is that good or bad?"

She gave me a sympathetic smile. "I guess that depends on who you ask. A lot of us, like me, I'm Fiona by the way, are happy that you're here. But we've also already heard about the meeting last night and your argument in the parking lot."

"Geez. Word gets around here fast, huh?"

"It's a small town." She shrugged. "You'll become used to it. But, between you and me, it's about time someone stood up to Annette. She's the worst." She looked over my shoulder and nodded.

I took that as my cue to leave. "It was nice to meet you. Have a great day."

I had been at the shop for two hours. I'd already arranged all the chairs and stands and was busy hanging artwork on the walls. The smell of fresh paint and the sound of music thumping through the speakers had elevated my mood drastically. I climbed up a step ladder to hang an award and heard a knock on the front door. I kept it locked while I was setting up so curious passersby wouldn't interrupt my process.

When I looked over, I was pleasantly surprised to see a man, about my age, standing there. He was handsome, with deep brown hair and brown eyes. We stared at each other for a moment before he reached up and tapped a badge against the glass in the door. I wasn't expecting that. In my rush to go unlock the door, I momentarily forgot I was on a ladder and stepped backwards. My heart jumped into my throat as I fell into the back of one of the chairs and slid almost to the floor.

I could feel my face redden from embarrassment. I opened the door and welcomed him in, hoping he didn't see my awkward dismount from the ladder.

"Are you okay? It looked like you may have twisted your ankle a bit."

My voice came out shaky. "I'm fine. Just a little embarrassed. I, um, forgot I was on a ladder. Thankfully, I was only on the bottom rung." I ran my fingers through my hair to give myself a moment to gather my thoughts. "What can I do for you?"

"I'm Detective Alex Landry. I came to ask you a few questions about the altercation you had with Maggie Scott last night."

"Who? Was that the girl in the parking lot?"

"Maggie Scott, yes. I heard you two had an argument after the meeting last night."

"Oh, my apologies. I never got her name. But why are you here because of an argument? I know it's a small town and all, but you must have better things to do with your time." I knew it sounded rude, but I couldn't stop the words from coming out.

Alex smiled but it wasn't friendly. "I don't investigate arguments. I do, however, investigate homicides."

I nearly choked on the air I was breathing in. "I'm sorry, I don't understand."

"Maggie Scott's body was found floating in the pool at the rec center this morning." He looked at me as if I should have known that information already.

"That's terrible. But may I ask why you're calling it a homicide? Wouldn't you assume she drowned?"

He raised his eyebrows. "Funny you would ask that question after claiming not to know her. Maggie was a competitive swimmer. The odds of her drowning are slim."

"Okay, but accidents do happen. I mean, it's still possible. Unless someone stabbed her or something."

He twisted up his mouth. "Now, why would you think she was stabbed?"

I couldn't help but roll my eyes. "All I'm saying is, regardless of her status as a swimmer, wouldn't the obvious conclusion be that she drowned if someone found her in a pool? The only reason one wouldn't assume that would be if she had another obvious cause of death, like a stab or gunshot wound or a strangulation mark. I just think it's weird that you're jumping to the conclusion that it's a homicide."

"I didn't realize that tattoo artists were also detectives, but I'll keep that in mind. What were you two arguing about?"

I was having trouble trying to figure out if he was being serious. "I'm not even sure you can call it an argument." I explained how she approached me and how our conversation played out. "And I just drove away. You can ask anyone who was at the meeting. I'm sure they all saw our interaction."

"I did ask other people. That's why I'm here." He shot me a look that told me he was looking for more information, but I didn't have any to give him. "Well, I know you just got here but as of right now, you're my prime suspect. Don't leave town."

Chapter 2

I worked for another hour not being able to get his words out of my head. *I was his prime suspect? Because of a conversation?* This was sure to get my name around town. It just wasn't the type of publicity I was hoping for.

I locked the door behind me and walked two buildings over to the diner. I had only been here once since I arrived and hadn't thought to bring any flyers with me on my first visit. I did notice they had a bulletin board in the entryway, so I made it a point to bring one with me this time.

I ordered a grilled ham and cheese sandwich to go and took in the atmosphere while I waited. It was too early for a lunch rush and too late for breakfast, but the dining area was still full. It wasn't even tourist season yet. I could understand the appeal as it had a welcoming vibe. Instrumental music hummed softly from the overhead speakers; the smell of bacon hung in the air. They had updated all the furniture and countertops since the last time I had visited as a child.

I walked over and pinned my flyer to the board while a woman with a name tag that read 'Temperance' set my order on the counter.

"You're Dakota?" Seeing the look on my face, she pointed toward my flyer. "I saw you in here the other day, but I didn't put it together. You've managed to create quite a reputation for yourself so far." She tried to give a friendly smile, but it was dripping with sympathy. I felt like I had gone through this exact same scenario at the coffee shop.

"So, I've heard." I sighed.

"I'm Temperance." She reached across the counter and shook my hand. "I'm sorry you seem to be having so much trouble, but I wouldn't worry too much about it. You have a lot of us in your corner."

"Well, I appreciate that. This isn't exactly the type of welcome I was expecting."

"Unfortunately, in a small town, many people are resistant to change. It'll blow over soon enough. But, hey, I'll see you this weekend. I have an appointment scheduled with you."

"Fantastic. I'll see you there." I took my sandwich and headed back to the shop wondering what she knew about my so-called reputation. *Was it my business, the run-in with Maggie, or the fact that I was the prime suspect in her murder?* Whichever it was, I was sure the entire town would know all about me soon enough.

For the second time that day, I heard a knock on the front door. Annoyed, I swore and walked from the back where I was busy organizing supplies. My mood immediately lightened when I saw Cheyenne waving at me through the glass. She was beaming.

I unlocked the door and she gave me the tightest hug. "I am so happy to see you." I felt instant relief at her touch. Cheyenne had an energy that people fed off. She was always friendly and upbeat, positive in every situation. We met a number of years ago when we both attended a tattoo convention. We were only apprentices at the time, but we had both gone on to open our own shops and make names for ourselves since then.

She held me at arm's length and stared at me for a moment. "You look amazing and I've missed you so much. Hey, did you know there's a rumor going around that you murdered someone?"

My face fell. "Yeah, I heard. I'm the prime suspect."

Cheyenne laughed. "Did you start that rumor yourself? You always did have the best marketing tactics."

"No. Unfortunately, I heard it directly from the detective." If I didn't feel so awful about the situation, I would have laughed at the look of shock on her face.

"Wait. You mean to tell me someone was actually murdered here?" Her eyes had doubled in size.

I nodded. "Yes. And I don't want to talk about it anymore. Come, look around. What do you think so far?" I had put in hours of work since I'd arrived and was so proud of how nicely the shop had come together.

I painted the walls a light, seafoam green and chose a dark gray for the accents and counters. The tiled floor was also a deep gray and together they had a calming effect. I painted my logo, a masquerade mask with satin behind the eyes, on the back wall so visitors would see it as soon as they entered the shop. I loved the aesthetic and hoped others would feel the same.

"It looks beautiful in here. I love the colors, they're very soothing. But didn't you say you have five guest artists? I only see three chairs and it's so small in here."

I nodded. "I have portable chairs in the back. And I scheduled it so only four of us will be tattooing at one time. I didn't think I would really need a big space since most of the time it'll be just me here." Cheyenne was right. As I looked at the space around me, I questioned whether I should have scheduled around three artists. "When did you get into town?"

"Last night, late."

"What do you say we finish sorting the supplies? Then, we can get an early dinner and I'll show you around a bit. I don't expect anyone else until tomorrow afternoon."

"Sounds good to me."

I woke up early again. No matter how hard I tried, I was never able to sleep past five. After taking Cheyenne for a brief tour around town last night, I dug through the boxes I had labeled as 'kitchen', putting dishes and utensils away as I went, to find my coffeemaker. I made myself a strong cup and took it out to my back porch.

I had gotten lucky with the location of my shop, but I felt like I won the lottery with my house. The town only afforded a view of the cabins and lake that drew in the summer tourists from three houses and mine was one of them. My backyard was small, butted against a dirt road that wound around the lake. I remembered riding my bike along that road during our vacations, hitting all the rivets and tire tracks, pedaling as fast as my legs could go to try to get a little bit of air. I chuckled at the thought, knowing back then I thought I was the next Evel Knievel, when the reality was, I probably never left the ground.

Mornings were still cold, but it was worth it to be outside, enjoying the quiet. Having spent so many years in the city, I had almost forgotten what silence was like. Here, there were no sirens, no arguments, no garbage trucks slamming heavy, metal bins around at five in the morning. The small-town atmosphere was peaceful with only the wind blowing through the trees and the birds chirping their 'good mornings'. A bang on my front door pulled me from my tranquil moment.

I sighed and made my way through the maze of boxes in my living room. "What the hell?" I unlocked the front door and swung it open. "Annette? It's six in the morning. What are you doing here?"

She stepped inside without waiting for an invitation. "Tell me why you did it." Her body was rigid, her words full of venom.

I made sure my filter was in place before responding. Speaking before I think is one of my worst personality traits. "Listen. I understand that you don't like me. Your reasoning is completely misguided but that's neither here nor there. To answer your question, I didn't do it. I also didn't invite you into my house, so you can go now." Still standing in the doorway, I swung my arm wide to show her the direction she should be going.

"Can't you just save everyone the time and trouble and admit that you murdered her so we can get this whole thing over with? Just make it easy for everyone involved."

I couldn't help but laugh at the absurdity of her request. "I'm not going to admit to something I didn't do just because you think it'll make you feel better. And I'm not going to ask you again, get out of my house."

"You need…"

"Out." It was a good thing I didn't have any close neighbors, that last word would have woken them all for sure.

Annette grunted and stepped outside, turning back to face me. "I'm not giving up."

I slammed the door in her face.

My morning of quiet and tranquility, so rudely interrupted, was gone. I took a quick shower and dressed for the day. I just began applying some makeup when I heard another knock on my door. I swore under my breath and prepared myself to see Annette's face again. It wasn't her. Alex Landry was standing on my front step.

"You look surprised to see me."

"No, I, yes." I paused and took a deep breath. "I thought you were Annette."

He squinted his eyes, confused. "Sorry to disappoint you. I have a couple of questions to ask you."

I sighed and opened the door wider for him to come in. "Excuse the boxes. I haven't had much time to unpack." I looked him up and down. It was a shame he was investigating me for murder. Every part of him, including the way he walked, was easy on the eyes and his voice, quiet and deep, was electrifying. "What can I help you with today?"

He held a piece of paper out to me. "You can start by telling me where you've been distributing these flyers."

My heart started to speed up, knowing he wasn't going to like what I had to tell him. "I've been posting those flyers everywhere. I even had some on my counter at my old shop."

"And by everywhere?"

"Everywhere. I only moved three hours away and it took me four days to get here. I hung one in every place I could think of."

"Mhm. And what about this one?" He pulled his phone from his pocket and showed me a quarter page flyer that only showed one piece of my flash art.

My brow furrowed. "I didn't distribute any of those." My mouth hung open as I tried to process how he would have gotten a copy of it. "Where did you get that?"

"I'm the one asking the questions here. Where would someone have gotten this flyer?"

"I don't know." My voice came out much sterner than I meant it to. "I only made one copy of each of those. They're for the grand opening of the shop." I had created twenty custom designs for our fifty-dollar flash pieces. My plan was to post them at the entrance of the shop so our clients could choose which one they wanted. My guest artists hadn't even seen them yet.

"Where is that copy now?"

"It's in a folder at the shop. I'm putting them on display tonight." He was nodding as I spoke but the look on his face told me he didn't believe a word I said. I rolled my eyes at him and made no attempt to try to hide it. "I was going to head over in a little while, but I guess I can go over now if you'd like to follow me and see for yourself."

"Thought you'd never ask. I'll wait outside."

I grunted as I watched him walk out the door. So much for my last bit of solitude for the next few days. I threw on a zip-up hoodie, grabbed my bag and car keys, and headed out the door. I didn't say a word to Alex as I walked by him on the way to my Jeep.

It felt weird having a detective following me and the ten minute drive to the shop felt more like thirty. I was used to living in a busy city where it was nearly impossible to even reach the speed limit, never mind exceed it. Here, in this quiet, laid-back town, it was just as impossible to go as slow as the posted limit.

I waited at the door of the shop until he joined me. I didn't want to give him any reason to think I was doing something wrong. I didn't know why but the presence of any law enforcement always made me feel like I was guilty of something, even when I knew I wasn't. It was probably a long-term side effect of my not so perfect teenage years. I dropped my keys on the counter and handed him the folder that was sitting on my laptop.

He opened it and fumbled for a moment, trying to keep the pages from flying out. "How many different ones did you have?"

"Twenty. All brand new line drawings for the opening." I watched as he set the folder down and began to count the number of pieces.

"Nineteen." He closed the folder and tucked it under his arm. "I'll be taking this for evidence." He started out the door before turning back. "How many people have been inside the shop since you got here?"

I smirked. "You."

"That's it?"

"And one of my guest artists. She was here yesterday."

"Does this guest artist have a name?"

I sighed for what felt like the twentieth time today and balled my hands into fists. "Cheyenne."

Chapter 3

Cheyenne banged on the shop door just before nine o'clock. She was bouncing up and down with what appeared to be a nervous energy. Her bouncing gained momentum the longer I took getting to the door. I unlocked it and she ripped it open, not waiting for an invitation to come in.

"Whoa. What's got into you this morning?"

"You're friend, Alex. He came to pay me a visit this morning." She looked and sounded like she was accusing me of sending him to see her. "Apparently, I'm also on his suspect list."

I couldn't help but laugh, not because it was funny but because it was so absurd for either of us to be on his list. "Welcome to the club."

"This isn't funny, Dakota. I'm a suspect in a murder."

I would have thought she was angry if it wasn't for the tears forming in her eyes. "In case you've forgotten, I'm not only on his list, I'm at the top of it. He was at my house before seven this morning." Cheyenne was staring at the ceiling, lost in thought. I wasn't sure she heard anything I had said. "Come, sit down with me for a minute. What did he have to say? Why does he think you could have had anything to do with it?"

"First, he asked me when I got into town. I told him it was two nights ago and then he asked me to tell him everywhere I have been since I got here. He showed me a picture of one of your flash pieces and asked me why I took it. He actually accused me of stealing your work." The words were tumbling out of her mouth as if she had no control over them.

"Take a deep breath. What did you tell him about the flash?"

"You know me. I'm always honest." She shrugged. "I told him I hadn't seen any of the drawings yet and that you were planning on showing all of us at the same time. But then..." Her voice trailed off, she took a deep breath and released it slowly, a tactic I had seen her use many times when she was stressed or felt overwhelmed. "Then he asked if I knew Maggie and I said 'no' because I didn't recognize her name. But I do know her, Dakota. Well... I did know her. He showed me her picture and he saw the look on my face when I realized who she was."

"Wait. You knew Maggie? How?"

"We went to high school together, only our freshman year, and then she moved away. I'm sure it goes without saying, we did not get along."

"Actually, you do need to say it. I only met her once." High school was over ten years ago for both of us. It was a little weird that they would run into each other now but things like that did happen. "But why would going to school with her matter now? That was so long ago."

Cheyenne shook her head. "I guess everything matters when a detective doesn't have any other solid evidence or leads."

I opened my mouth to speak but closed it again and stared at the logo on my wall. "You know what? If he doesn't have any evidence or clues as to who killed her, I'm going to help him get some." I stood and grabbed my keys off the counter. "Let's go get some coffee."

"Hey, Fiona." The coffee shop was still busy. Nearly every table was taken, most filled with laptops and people talking on their phones. It wasn't the quietest place to work but the atmosphere probably drew most people in. The shop had low lighting and dark, wood trim. The tables and chairs were tall with black, metal legs and heavily varnished, thick, wooden tops. It smelled of a mix of sweet pastries and freshly brewed coffee. The far walls were exposed brick and the counter was in the middle of the room rather than being pushed against a wall like most.

"Dakota, hi. The usual?"

"Yes, please. Plus, whatever she'd like." She set our coffees on the counter and I gestured for her to meet me at the other end. "I know we only just met but I was hoping you might be able to tell me if you heard anything more about Maggie Scott." I grimaced as soon as the words left my mouth.

"Yeah, quite a bit, actually. Annette has been going practically door to door asking what people know about you."

"Huh. And here I thought she had already formed her opinion of me."

Fiona gave me a sympathetic look again. "Oh, she has. While she's inquiring about you, she's also trying to persuade people to agree with her feelings about you. I also heard you and your friend are suspects. Is that part true?"

I nodded. "Unfortunately, it is. Apparently, it's not safe to disagree with someone or to have gone to high school with them."

"Geez, sorry you're going through this. I'm sure you have enough to worry about with your opening and all."

"You could say that. I really appreciate you filling me in." I turned to leave but heard her call my name.

"Dakota?" She gestured for me to come back to the counter and whispered. "You didn't hear it from me, but you might want to accidentally run into Leyland. I heard this morning that he's back in town. Him and Maggie dated a few years ago."

"Thank you."

Cheyenne and I parted ways. She went back to the hotel to rest for a few hours and I took a drive to the next town over to pick up some refreshments for the arrival of the rest of my guest artists. I also needed to reprint my flash art photos.

All my artists were expected to arrive in the early evening and we planned to meet at the shop at six. My plan for the night was simple. I wanted to welcome everyone, introduce them to each other, and let them know what their schedules looked like for the next four days. I would show them the flash art pieces that we were offering and then I would feed them and we would socialize for a few hours. It was supposed to be an easy, carefree night before the events of the next four days.

Now, I had to decide whether I wanted to fill them in on what was going on in case they heard the rumors circulating or if Alex decided to pay a visit to the shop again. Thankfully, the forty-five minute drive to town gave me plenty of time to consider the pros and cons of telling them.

The drive also gave me time to try to think of a way to clear both mine and Cheyenne's names from Alex's suspect list. I knew the first thing I had to do was figure out who Leyland was. I needed to find out who Maggie swam for if she really was a competitive swimmer. I already knew I would have to get creative since I could hardly just walk into the rec center and start asking questions. One piece of information I did have was that I didn't see Cheyenne until yesterday and the flash art had to have been taken the night before. I didn't think Alex would believe me for a minute about it being impossible for her to have gotten it, but I had to at least try.

The task of clearing my own name would be much easier if I knew more people in town. At the very least, it would be helpful if I knew who I could trust. I needed to know for sure who broke into my shop and stole my flash piece and what kind of motive they had for doing it. Did people really have such strong opposition to my being here that they were willing to frame me for murder? The logical conclusion to that question was 'yes' but the more pressing question was why someone would want Maggie Scott dead. And why were they going through all the trouble of trying to frame someone for murder when they could just as easily have made it look like an accident? I needed to find a way to befriend Alex so I could get some answers to my questions.

By the time I got back to town, I had less than five hours before I needed to be back at the shop. I tried to save a little time by buying a quick lunch and eating it on the drive home. I didn't eat fast food often, but it was convenient every once in a while.

I stopped at home and put the drinks and sandwiches in the refrigerator before making a stop at the shop to put up two small, motion activated cameras. I put one above the front door and one on the back. I didn't plan on having to add any sort of security features but after the last two days, I figured something simple couldn't hurt.

After mounting my own cameras, I drove over to the rec center just to have a quick look around. I wondered if they had any security cameras set up and I couldn't quite remember how close the other buildings were to it. I hadn't been to this area of town in years except for the meeting the other night, but I drove straight to the town hall and straight out. I didn't know if they had built it up at all.

A wave of nostalgia hit me every time the fountain came into view. Coming here was my favorite part of my summer vacations. Of course, I missed my friends but after a day or two, I didn't want to leave. All the town buildings were situated around the green. I didn't take any notice of the other buildings when I was here the other night. I had parked in the lot between the library and town hall and had taken the most direct route to and from. If I had taken the longer way around the green, I would have passed the rec center, schools, police and fire stations, and the hotel, which was the only locally owned business on this side of town.

I drove into the parking lot I was in the other night and slowly made my way around the perimeter, looking for cameras or anything else that may catch my eye. Finding nothing, I moved on to the schools and finally the rec center. Coming from the city, it was weird to not see a single camera. I had gotten so used to them being on almost every building I didn't even notice them anymore.

Crime scene tape wrapped around the entrance to the rec center. I was hoping I would be able to go in and take a look around, but I would have to wait. I didn't want anyone to find me breaking and entering or disturbing an active crime scene. That was the last thing I needed. I was already in enough trouble and I hadn't even done anything.

Another car pulled into the parking lot and parked. A woman, about my age, got out, swung a gym bag over her shoulder, and started toward the building. Her head was down, focused on the phone in her hand. She walked right up until she almost ran into the yellow and black tape, before taking a step back. Her shoulders sagged and she turned and started back to her car.

I put my own car in park and scrambled out of the driver's seat. I half-walked, half-ran toward her. "Excuse me?"

She hesitated and turned toward me. Her hair was pulled back in a tight bun and she wore yoga pants and a sports jacket.

"The center is closed."

"Yeah, I can see that."

I needed a minute to think of a few questions I could ask her. I wasn't planning to run into anyone. "Do you have any idea when it's supposed to open again? I'd, uh, like to be able to use the pool until the lake warms up a little."

For the first time, she looked directly at me. Her stare was hard and cold. "Do you think I'm stupid, Dakota?"

I took a step back. "I'm sorry, do I know you?"

"The important thing is, I know you. It's your fault the center isn't open. And I don't appreciate you talking to Fiona about Maggie." She shifted her gym bag higher on her shoulder.

"How do you know I talked to Fiona?"

She rolled her eyes and huffed. "I work at the coffee shop. I've seen you there the past two days."

"You'll probably see me there every day. I work right across the street."

"Not for long, you won't. You murdered my best friend and you won't get away with it." She opened her driver's door, threw her bag across the front seat, and drove away, leaving me standing alone in the middle of the parking lot.

I never got her name, but it would be easy enough to figure out. And I wasn't quite sure what the feeling of uneasiness meant, but I did know there was something about the way she said "best friend" that told me they might have been anything but.

Chapter 4

I swung home to pick up the food and went over to the shop. I put the new copies of my flash art in some frames and set up a folding table in the middle of the room. I was setting out the food when I heard a knock on the front door. I expected a couple of artists to arrive a few minutes early but almost forty-five minutes was borderline rude.

I took a deep breath and turned toward the door. Fiona's red hair was the first thing I noticed. I unlocked the door and stepped aside so she could come in and locked the door behind her.

"I'm really sorry to bother you. I won't take up much of your time. Wow. This is a beautiful color."

I watched as she took the entire shop in. "Thank you. I find it calming. And it's no problem, I was just setting up for a meeting. I'm expecting the rest of my artists tonight. What's up?"

"I wanted to talk to you for a minute and kind of... warn you, I guess. Carly came back to work a few hours after she left, sweating and tense because she ran into you outside the rec center. I don't know what you did, I don't really talk to her very often, you know, other than work stuff, but I think she may have gone to the police station."

"Great. So, I guess I should be waiting for Alex to come banging on my door again. But, what would she have to tell anyone? I only talked to her for a minute."

Fiona frowned. "Dakota? You only talked to Maggie for a minute."

I sighed loudly. "Why is everyone in this town so caught up with me?"

"Because. You're going to hear this excuse over and over again, this is a small town. People who live here don't like change. Life is different here. A lot of the locals, the people who were born here, they view this town as being very wholesome. Things like tattoos and motorcycles are still taboo to them. A consequence of never having left town for more than a day or two. But, don't worry too much about it. As soon as the next interesting thing happens, they'll forget all about you." Her face contorted when she realized what she said. "I didn't mean it that way. I just meant the ridiculous amount of negative attention will be someone else's to deal with."

I had to laugh at how she stumbled. "It's okay. I know what you meant. I have to be honest and tell you I'm almost looking forward to people forgetting about me and I've only been here for three days."

Fiona chuckled. "Well, I won't keep you any longer. Like I said, I just wanted to give you the head's up."

I thanked her and walked her out. No sooner had I made it back to the table before the first knock sounded on the door. Cheyenne. I ushered her through the door. "Oh, I'm so glad it's you. Real quick before the others get here, Fiona just stopped by to tell me Carly went to the police station after I met her today. I'm surprised Alex hasn't busted through the door yet."

"Me too. Who's Carly?"

"Sorry. I forgot I haven't spoken to you. I just met her today. Apparently, she's Maggie's best friend. Well...was anyway." As expected, as soon as I finished my sentence the next knock echoed through the shop. I couldn't wait to be open for business so I didn't have to hear people knocking anymore.

Once everyone arrived, I thanked them all for agreeing to come to my opening as guest artists and introduced them all to each other. Some had already met, others hadn't. Between them, Cheyenne, Willow, Sierra, Dallas, and Riley, it seemed they would all get along just fine. I showed them the schedule for the next four days and right before I was going to show them the flash art pieces, as I imagined would happen, Alex tapped on the glass.

I grunted and opened the door. "I had a feeling I might see you."

"Oh, yeah? Why is that?"

"Just, give me a minute, okay?" I turned toward my guests to apologize for the interruption. I handed the first piece of flash art to Cheyenne and asked her to pass them around. "I made twenty pieces that our clients can choose from. I plan to display them along the front counter so they can see them as soon as they walk in." I excused myself and turned my attention to Alex.

"I thought I would see you since I ran into Carly today. I heard she went looking for you after."

"Oh, she did. Mind telling me why you're following her?"

I had to laugh. "I didn't follow her. I was in the parking lot first and until I met her there, I didn't even know she existed." I sounded defensive. It was one thing for people to form an opinion, no matter how unfounded it may be, but it was a completely different story when someone went out of their way to twist the details.

"She said you put cameras up. Are you spying on her?"

"You've got to be kidding me. I already told you; I just met her this afternoon. I also didn't know that she worked at the coffee shop until we had our conversation. I had already put the cameras up by then."

"Mhm. And what made you put up security cameras?"

"I put them up because someone was clearly in here. I know Cheyenne didn't steal my artwork and I have a feeling it probably wasn't you."

"Speaking of, you told me you only had one set printed but," he gestured around the room, "it looks to me like you lied because you seem to have a second set."

I shook my head. "I printed this set this morning when I went into town. You took my only copy and I needed one for the opening tomorrow." Seeing the look on his face I walked behind the counter and dug through my bag. "Here. This is the receipt from the print shop. You can see both the time and date right here."

He looked at it and handed it back to me. "Why were you at the rec center?"

I tried but quickly realized I didn't have any patience left for him. "Listen. I know you have a job to do and you've made it clear that I'm your prime suspect. I don't expect you to try to help me, but I'll be damned if I don't try to help myself. So, while you're busy looking for things to make me seem guilty, I know I'm innocent and I'm going to do everything in my power to prove it to you."

"Stay clear of my crime scenes and keep your nose out of business that isn't yours." He turned and walked out without another word.

It was only once I locked the door that I could feel everyone's eyes on me. I turned around and smiled. "I guess I can't hide it from all of you anymore, huh?" I was in a room full of people shaking their heads. "Okay. If you haven't heard yet, there are a number of people in this town who are anything but happy that I'm here. Yesterday morning, someone killed a woman, around my age, and a lot of residents, including the detective who was just here, think I'm guilty. Obviously, it wasn't me, but my word isn't enough to change any of their opinions." I stopped talking to give anyone who wanted to a chance to respond. They all just stared at me in an uncomfortable silence. "All right, well...I'm not sure if no immediate reaction is good or bad, but if you have any questions, I'll answer them the best I'm able.

"Going back to the flash art, you all know how it works. Make each piece your own but keep time and cost in mind." I pointed toward the food. "If you guys are hungry, feel free to help yourselves."

All of them got up and filled a plate and got something to drink. Sierra was the only one who came over to talk to me.

"Dakota, your shop looks amazing. And the color scheme screams your style."

"Thank you." I gave her a huge grin. "I'm glad you like it."

"I really do." She nodded. "I'm sure you don't want to hear about this or talk about it, but just so you know, I already heard about that dead girl today. A couple people in the diner down the road were talking about you."

I grunted. "I just really hope this doesn't affect our appointments. If people cancel on me, I'd understand, but I hope it doesn't happen to any of you."

"Oh, I didn't even think about that. Have you had any cancellations yet?"

"Well, no, not yet. Oddly enough, I've had people call requesting appointments. I had to put them on the wait list."

She looked at me with wide eyes and a cocked head. "Why don't you just extend the grand opening pricing and schedule them in next week? Uh, I'm sorry. That was rude. I didn't mean to question how you're running your own business."

"That's okay. If I were you, I would have suggested the same thing. But the truth is… remember when I asked you to come out here and you asked how I would be able to do this financially? I'm booked out six months in advance."

Her jaw dropped. "Tell me you're kidding?"

I shook my head. "Afraid not. Apparently, a lot of my clients will look for any reason to book a two or three day vacation."

Sierra looked like she was going to fall over. Instead, she leaned forward and rested her hand on my shoulder. "I am so proud of you."

I awoke feeling both anxious and excited. I drank a cup of coffee and showered. Since I didn't have anything else planned, I decided to stop by the coffee shop and then my shop to double check that everything was ready to go. I believed the only thing left to set up was the last table and then I would be able to enjoy a few quiet hours.

The drive over to the shop was never what I would consider busy but this morning it was eerily quiet. I usually saw at least four or five cars, but no one seemed to be around today. I pulled up to the stop sign across from the shop and my jaw dropped. For a moment, what I was seeing didn't seem real. The entire front of my building was spray painted with the word "murderer" in all capital letters and bright red paint.

I parked my car on the side of the shop, walked to the front door, and pulled out my phone. The last thing I wanted to do was deal with Alex this morning, but I didn't see any other choice. After calling the police station, I snapped a few pictures with my phone. Not only did they get the front of the shop, but they tagged one side of my a-frame sign as well. I wanted to turn it around so the painted side wouldn't show but I decided to wait for Alex so he could see it first. I was so glad I chose to fill my guests in last night. At least this wouldn't come as a complete shock.

Alex and Fiona arrived at the same time. "Dakota? I'm so sorry someone did this to you." Fiona was shaking her head, looking at the mess in the front of my building. "I can't stay but I thought you could use some coffee. Let me know if you need anything, okay?" She handed me the cup and went back across the street to the coffee shop.

"I see you found a friend. That's nice." Alex hadn't even looked in my direction. He was too busy taking his own pictures of my shop.

"Believe it or not, there are a few people who actually like me."

He looked at me out of the corner of his eye, brow raised, and gestured toward the building. "Yeah. Looks like it."

My filter all but disappeared. "Listen. I really couldn't care less if you like me or not. But you're still an officer and regardless of how you feel about me, someone vandalized my property and I expect you to do your job, bias aside."

"I know how to do my job without emotional attachment." He had made his way to the front door and was taking pictures of the lock.

"We'll see about that."

He finally looked at me straight on. "Do you always speak to members of law enforcement this way?"

"You know, it's not often I have run-ins with the law but the few times I have, the assertive nature of my words wasn't warranted." I stared straight at him, daring him to argue with me.

He didn't argue, he just rolled his eyes. "So, you set up cameras yesterday. Have you checked the footage yet?"

"Not yet. I only arrived a few minutes before you. Can we go inside? It'll probably be easier to see on my laptop." He nodded and I unlocked the door. We both waited patiently while the laptop booted up and I logged in to the security system.

"Right there." Alex pointed to the screen and I slowed down the video speed.

"Of course. They're wearing a baseball cap and a hoodie."

"Well, I'll give you credit for one thing. Even though whoever did this put effort into hiding their identity, you do have an eye for quality tech."

I curled up one side of my mouth. "I'll accept your compliment when I get your apology speech for not believing me."

He stood up straight, dropped his business card on the counter, and headed for the door. "I'll expect a copy of that video in my email before I get back to the station."

Chapter 5

All five of my artists showed up at exactly nine-thirty. Riley and Dallas were immersed in conversation; neither seemed to notice the front of the building. The other three walked right up to me and began bombarding me with questions and smothering me with sympathy. I had to ask them all to give me a little space and then excused myself. I didn't do well being the center of attention. Some people lived for stuff like that, but it made me uncomfortable and I couldn't handle it for more than a minute or two.

"Dallas? I'm sorry for the interruption but did you just say 'Leyland'?"

She nodded. "I did. He's so good-looking. Tall, strong, you know my type. I..."

"Yeah, yeah. Where was he? Did you just see him this morning?"

She curled up her lip in annoyance. "Yeah. He's in the diner right now. We just..."

"I'll be right back." I ran out the door without any further information. I would have to be sure to apologize to her when I got back. Thankful for the small town setup, I ran the two doors down to the diner. I whipped the door open and stood just inside, surveying the room. I didn't have a plan for what to do if I found him. Just as my eyes locked on who I could only assume was Leyland, I heard Temperance calling my name.

"Hey, I'm sorry. This is so rude of me. I didn't actually come in to order any food. Um, someone told me I should talk to Leyland and I heard he was here? I kind of just wanted to see what he looked like so I would be able to spot, and hopefully, talk to him later. I don't have time to talk to him now. We're supposed to be opening in twenty minutes." I felt bad. All she said was my name and I poured half my life story out to her. "Sorry about all that. I think I'm a little overwhelmed this morning.

"It's okay. I understand. That gentleman you were just looking at is Leyland. He's nice, definitely the black sheep of his family. So you can find him later, his last name is Bailey. I'll warn you, though, you may want to stay clear of his sister, Laura. She doesn't exactly play nice with others."

"Thank you. I've gotta...," I pointed to the door and she nodded to show her understanding.

"Of course. Go. I'll see you this afternoon."

When I got back to the shop I had just enough time to apologize to everyone before all four of our first appointment clients showed up and gathered outside the door.

The first six hours flew by. We had the radio on, all the clients and artists were having great conversations, and we hadn't had a single cancellation or no-show yet. All the other artists had gotten at least one break so far. I had one client left before I was scheduled for a break and I was grateful because I was starting to get hungry.

I looked up to see a man enter the shop. I had only managed to get a glimpse of the side of his face in the diner but there was no mistaking it. Leyland Bailey just walked into my shop. I stood to greet him. "Hi. Can I help you?"

He ran his fingers through his hair, telling me he was a bit uncomfortable. "Hey. Um. This is a bit awkward but, uh, Maggie had an appointment with you, but, um, before she died, she told me she changed her mind and said I could take her spot." He pulled his shoulders to his ears and let them drop again.

I wasn't sure how to respond. This situation was something I didn't even think I could make up. "I don't think I had an appointment with her. Let me double check." I looked over my schedule while he stood just inside the door, awkwardly looking around. "What time was her appointment supposed to be?"

"Now." He reached into his back pocket and pulled out a small planner. "She left this at my house the other day." He turned to the current date and showed it to me.

Simple but precise.

Tattoo. 4pm with Dakota.

"That's weird. I have an appointment at that time but it's with a Veronica Tandy. Give me just a few minutes to see if Veronica shows. If she doesn't, I'll fit you in. In the meantime, go ahead and choose which piece you'd like."

He slid the planner back into his pocket and did a quick sweep across the counter with his eyes, not looking directly at any of the choices.

I gave my scheduled client ten more minutes and busied myself setting up my station before calling Leyland back. "I guess you're getting a tattoo." I didn't mind as much since the flash pieces were small, simple designs and each client could choose whichever they wanted, but people switching or giving away appointments wasn't something I would typically allow, especially last minute.

Having an appointment set up meant I was creating a unique piece, specifically for that client. I always waited until that morning to put the finishing touches on the drawing and that allowed me to focus on the style and design they wanted and to tailor the appointment to cost. Switching my mindset last minute didn't ever allow for the best outcomes and many times it altered the price and my scheduled timeline for the day. I didn't think I would have to worry about it here but at my old shop, it was a policy that was strictly adhered to.

He chose my favorite piece out of the ones I was offering and it was the first time I got to do it all day. I designed a monkey face coming out of the top of a banana peel and I kind of wanted it for myself because it was so cute.

"So, I heard you just got back to town. Were you traveling?"

"I just got back last week. I actually moved away for a few years."

"Oh? What made you come back?" I thought my simple questions might prompt answers that I could dive deeper into.

"I grew up here. I was starting to get bored so I moved to a much larger town for a change of pace. Turns out, I really missed the small town life. I have a really good job where I can work from home, so I decided to move back." I could tell by his speech that he had relaxed a lot since he first walked through the door. It usually worked the opposite way when I was tattooing; the longer they sat, the more tense they became.

"That's certainly convenient. I just arrived a few days ago myself. I have to assume job opportunities around here are limited."

He nodded his head and we sat through a few minutes of silence. I kept pushing through, wanting this tattoo to be over, but also wanting answers to more questions that I hadn't thought of yet.It was no surprise to me that he chose the same piece of artwork that had been found in Maggie's belongings when she was found and I wanted to know why.

"So, how'd you know Maggie? Did you grow up together?"

"We went to high school together. We also dated for about three years. I really loved her."

Asking about Maggie was uncomfortable and felt intrusive. The message scrawled across the front of my building only made it worse. "I'm sorry for your loss. I'm sure this can't be easy for you." I watched his face and saw no change in his expression. "I'm curious, substituting appointments isn't something we typically do. Did she happen to tell you why she changed her mind?"

"She didn't. I only saw her once since I got back. I mentioned that I wanted to make an appointment and she just offered me hers. I didn't know you frowned upon switching with someone, but it did feel weird coming in under the circumstances."

"Did she happen to mention which tattoo she was planning to get?" I stopped tattooing and looked him straight in the eye when I asked the question.

He hesitated to answer. "No. She just told me I could have her spot."

As soon as we finished, I cleaned up my station, rushed out to my car, and pulled out my phone. "Hey, it's Dakota. Where are you?"

Alex was waiting in the parking lot when I pulled in at the library. He was leaning against his car with his arms crossed over his chest and his feet crossed at the ankles. For the first time, I noticed how physically attractive he really was. He was the epitome of tall, dark, and handsome. His chestnut brown hair was short and swept to the side on top, his eyes were a deep shade of brown that one could easily get lost in, and his strength was highlighted by the way he was standing, his sleeves pulled tight on his biceps. I could only imagine how I might feel if he didn't suspect me of murder.

I didn't bother to make sure I appropriately parked in a spot. I pulled in next to him and got out. "Thank you for waiting for me. I have some information you might be interested in."

"I doubt it. While I can understand your desire to prove your innocence, I know how to do my job."

I could appreciate his position. I know I wouldn't want a client coming in and telling me how to do my job. "I'm not doubting your ability. If you already have this information, great, but if not, it may help. Since you waited, will you at least hear me out?"

He nodded his head once. "Go ahead."

I filled him in on my theory that Maggie had booked an appointment for a tattoo under a fake name. I relayed all the information Leyland had given me, including the fact that he saw her the night before they found her and he had her planner. "And, this could just be coincidental, but without even looking at the choices of flash art, he chose the exact piece that you found with Maggie's stuff. If nothing else, you have to find that extremely odd."

He raised his eyebrows and shook his head. "It's not that odd. They dated. They probably have similar likes and interests. But I'll talk to him."

"That's all I'm asking." I got in my car, satisfied not only that he listened, but because he all but admitted I handed him new information. My stomach grumbled as I drove back to the shop. In my hurry to meet Alex, I didn't stop to eat and now I was regretting that decision. Fortunately, I only had one appointment left for the day. Temperance was there, waiting for me, when I arrived back at the shop.

Temperance was easily fifteen years my senior but she didn't act like it. After this problem with Maggie is over, I feel like we'll be friends despite our age difference. I told her about my appointment with Leyland.

"I don't think he ever really got over Maggie. I heard he took their breakup really hard and he did move away a few weeks after it happened. Now that it's been a few years, maybe he thought moving back would give them a chance to reconcile."

"What if he asked her to give him another chance when he saw her the other day and she said 'no'? Do you think he would be capable of harming her?" I could almost see the wheels turning in her head.

She nodded. "Come to think of it, yes, it's quite possible. While I do my best to stay away from the entire family, I do remember hearing stories of him getting into a lot of fights when he was in high school. Physical ones. There was even a point when his parents threatened to send him off to boarding school if he didn't straighten out."

"That bad, huh?" I watched her face scrunch up as I hit a sensitive spot on her ankle bone. She opted for the appletini which was an oddly shaped apple with a glass stem protruding from the bottom and its leaf positioned as the garnish on the top. "Did things get any better?"

"Well, to my knowledge, he was never shipped off anywhere so I'm guessing the threats worked."

"I thought you told me earlier that he was really nice?"

"Oh, he is. He's always been pleasant to speak to, even as a teenager. By far, he's the most respectful member of his family. But I can only go on what I've heard and what I've witnessed. He's never been anything but nice and respectful toward me, but I've heard he can have a temper." She was silent for a few minutes. "Hey, I know a guy who can help to fix the front of your shop."

My eyes widened and I felt a figurative weight lift off my shoulders. "Really? That would be great. I still have to wait for Alex to give me the all-clear but I'd love some help fixing it."

Before she left, Temperance invited all of us to the diner, offering to open it just for us. She left with the promise of a sandwich spread and a couple soup and side options. I still hadn't eaten and I wasn't about to turn down her offer.

When we finished with our last clients, everyone pitched in to clean up the shop and we made our way over to the diner to get something to eat. Temperance welcomed and greeted us like we were all close friends. She had pulled two tables together and had dishes arranged on them in a buffet style.

Not having eaten anything all day, I made no apologies in grabbing a plate and being first in line. Once we were all settled and everyone was able to take a few bites of food, all the artists took out their phones and showed off their favorite pieces of the day. It was always fun to see how many different interpretations there were of the same line drawing. Even though we were only offering a few, simple flash pieces, it was clear from seeing the photos that I had gathered a group of extremely talented individuals. It made me feel even better about my choices hearing which design was their favorite because it showed how diverse we all were in our styles. Of the twenty pieces offered, I liked the banana monkey, Sierra preferred the turtle carrying a bindle, Willow chose the raspberry wearing a bikini, and the other three liked ant with the top hat, the teacup on a flying saucer, and the alien with a cat face.

It felt so good to sit down, relax, and chat with friends. I hadn't realized how much I needed it until Willow sidetracked the conversation.

"Dakota?"

Everyone stopped and stared at her due to the concern in her voice.

"I don't mean to kill the mood here and I know you're still mostly new to the area, but I have to ask, how well do you know the people in this town?"

"Well, you've met what, six, seven people today? I'd say you know about as many people as I do." I shrugged to let her know my number was as accurate as I could get. "I don't know anyone very well yet."

"Huh. I had a client earlier today, nice but not super talkative. About half-way through our session, completely out of the blue, she looked at me and said, 'Just so you know, I'm on Dakota's side.' At first, I thought she was talking about you opening the shop, so I smiled but didn't say anything. But she followed it up by saying, 'She was an awful person.' I realized she wasn't talking about the shop, but when I asked, she wouldn't elaborate anymore."

"What does that even mean? What side is she on?" I could only assume she was talking about Maggie. But does that mean this person also thought I was guilty of murder? And if so, she still came to my shop, kept her appointment, and it didn't bother her at all that she thought I murdered someone? Or did it mean she was on my side and believed I was innocent? "Who were you talking to?"

Willow took out her phone and thumbed through her schedule for the day. "She told me she works at the gift shop. Her name is...Karen Ryan."

Chapter 6

My head was spinning when I got home. We had a successful day at the shop, but I always find it exhausting when I have a full house from the moment I open until the time the shop closes. While I am thankful none of my clients cancelled, my day was more stressful due to all the activity surrounding Maggie's death. Each of my personal clients wanted to ask about Maggie. I can understand the curiosity, but the questions made me uncomfortable in the place I would normally find the most comfort. I felt like I was having to defend myself all day even though the questions were innocent. After Willow shared her client experience, everyone else chimed in to share theirs, as well. I knew people were talking about me, but I didn't realize until then that I was truly the talk of the town.

I curled up on my couch with a cup of tea, fighting the urge to call Matthew. I knew he would answer his phone, he always did. He would listen to me whine about my day and he'd give me the best advice he could come up with for how to work through this challenge. I told myself numerous times I wouldn't call him again once I moved. Matthew and I broke up eight months ago, no hard feelings on either side. We both agreed it would be best. After four years of being together, it proved a lot harder than either of us expected. Even though we lived together and spoke on the phone every night, we only saw each other once a month. We came to a mutual agreement that we both deserved more but it was a challenge to move on and each of us looked for reasons to reach out to the other. It didn't make our breakup any easier.

I picked up my phone twice to call him and set it back down, instead opting to have a fictitious conversation in my head. What would he tell me to do? I came to the conclusion that what I was doing was correct. My main focus needed to be my business but if I intended to keep the shop thriving, I needed to clear my name.

I had just settled down in bed when my phone pinged indicating I had a message.

Matthew.

HOW'D IT GO TODAY?
THE OPENING WAS SUCCESSFUL. THE REST OF THE DAY WAS NOT.
DO YOU WANT TO TALK?
NO. BUT THANK YOU FOR THE OFFER.
I'M HERE IF YOU CHANGE YOUR MIND. CONGRATS ON THE OPENING.

He ended his message with a kiss emoji and I chose not to reply. I knew if I did, the desire to hear his voice would be too great to resist. I set my phone back on the nightstand and fell asleep thinking about Matthew rather than my current dilemma.

All of us had just settled down with our first clients of the day when Alex walked into the shop. He didn't say anything, just stood inside the door, scanning the room. I rolled my eyes and went back to tattooing. If he didn't want to talk, I wasn't going to force him.

I could feel the eyes of my artists and clients alike on me and I shook my head. The room was silent except for the buzz of tattoo machines. There was a tension that seemed to occupy every square inch of space and smothered my concentration. I set my machine down and pulled off my gloves. Leaning against the back of my chair, arms crossed and eyebrows raised, I stared at Alex, waiting for him to speak.

He glanced at me from the corner of his eye and then zeroed in on one of my artists. "Riley Farris?"

She finished the line she was pulling and looked up at him. "Yes?"

"I need to ask you a few questions about your relationship with Maggie Scott."

"Who?"

My mouth fell open and all eyes slowly crept her way. A few people gasped when she indicated she didn't know who Maggie was.

"Maybe we should find a quieter place to talk?" Alex looked in my direction and I sighed.

"You can use the back room." I indicated with a quick nod of my head and he returned the gesture with a nod of appreciation.

Riley and Alex walked to the back and the rest of us went back to work. While they were gone, there was minimal chatter among us. For some, I believed it was the uncomfortable feeling. For others, like me, they were hoping to be able to hear even the shortest bit of what Riley and Alex were saying. It felt like they had been gone for hours but with a quick glance at my phone, I saw it had been just over ten minutes before they emerged.

Riley's face was bright red, enough to completely cover the sprinkle of freckles across her cheeks. She locked eyes with me as she sat down. I couldn't tell if she was angry or on the verge of tears. I hadn't noticed Alex was still leaning against the doorframe to the back room until I heard him call my name.

I sighed again and rolled my eyes before excusing myself from my client. I spun around before the door had even shut. "You do realize this is my opening weekend, right?" I crossed my arms over my chest. "It's not like everyone doesn't know what's going on but your presence is a huge disruption in my ability to run this business. Could you not have come to see us before we opened or waited until we had a break from clients?" My voice was louder than I intended but I didn't care. I was supposed to be finding a way to get him on my side, but he found a way to make me angry every time he came around.

Alex stood staring at me, no doubt trying to figure out how to approach the answer to my outburst. "Well, for starters, that's not how this works. In case you've forgotten, you're a suspect in a murder and I ask the questions. I don't need to ask for your permission."

"Fine. What can I do for you today, sir?"

"You can start by telling me how you chose your artists for the opening."

I almost thought he was joking but the look on his face told me otherwise. "They're all artists that I met while I was doing my apprenticeship. We've kept in touch and I thought it would be nice to give them guest spots. Cheyenne and I are close friends and we both own our own shops. The others haven't advanced quite as far in their career and this is a step in helping them to move forward."

He raised his eyebrows and tilted his head like he didn't believe me. "Did they ask you if they could come or did you reach out to them?"

"I asked them. Why did you need to talk to Riley?"

"If you really don't know the answer to that, you should go buy a lottery ticket because you certainly know how to pick them."

"What is that even supposed to mean? It doesn't make any sense." My heart was pounding and my muscles felt weak. I couldn't decipher whether it was nerves or anger.

"You have, what, five artists filling in here?"

"Yes. But they're not filling in, they're guests."

"Whatever. Out of five artists, what are the odds that two of them know the victim? That's one hell of a coincidence if you ask me."

All I could do was stare at him, sure I had the deer in the headlights look. I felt like I was going to fall over. I tried to speak but all that came out was a garbled sound from the bottom of my throat.

"You really didn't know?"

Not trusting my voice, I shook my head.

The shop was silent when I stepped out to the floor. If I couldn't see the clients and artists, I would have thought they all left. I sat back in my chair and picked up my machine but no one else moved. They didn't watch me walk through the shop. All eyes were on Alex as if he became the number one enemy. Maybe I had more friends here than I thought.

Alex wound his way around the shop instead of simply walking straight out the door. He stopped at the front counter and called my name again. "Can you come here for a minute?"

Not seeing that I had any other choice, I joined him.

"Care to tell me where this came from?" He pointed toward a drawer that was barely open. Hanging out was a gold, puffed heart pendant that I had never seen before.

I looked into his eyes and didn't know what to say. I had to fight to get any words to come out, knowing the longer I stayed quiet, the more guilty it would make me look. "I have no idea. I've never seen it."

"But it's in your shop, in your desk. You don't have any idea how it got here?"

"No, I don't."

I looked around the shop and everyone was wide eyed, staring at the pendant.

"This looks like a description I received of a necklace Maggie wore every day. I was told it was missing."

I went into a defensive mode again. "Do you have any idea how many people have been in this shop over the last two days? Half the town has been here. Anyone could have put it there."

"Yup." He pulled the drawer out, took a tissue from his pocket, and plucked the pendant out before wrapping it and putting it in his pocket. "Have a nice day." He left without another word.

I needed a break. As soon as I was able, I walked across the street to get some coffee. I was so thankful for the timing of having a lease become available where it did. I would have fought to get a lease either next to or across from the coffee shop if I had to. I felt a large amount of tension leave my body as soon as I opened the door and the smell of freshly ground coffee engulfed me. I took a deep breath and thought for sure I could feel it cleansing my soul.

As I approached the counter, I was grateful for that moment of Zen, no matter how brief it may have been. I locked eyes with Carly and saw Annette turn to look at me. It went without saying what they were talking about. Their eyes burned into me as I made my way to the counter.

I was never one to be violent, but I had definitely been known for my short temper since my early teenage years. Fortunately, as I matured into adulthood, I became more aware of my ability to control it. Instead of calling them out, I greeted Fiona and engaged in conversation while she rang up my order. She promised to fill me in later on anything she heard and we exchanged phone numbers.

I didn't expect my next scheduled client for another fifty minutes, so I made myself comfortable at the front counter. I had a client coming in on Wednesday for a large piece and I hadn't had a chance to start the drawing yet. I barely pulled up the reference photos when I heard a low rumble off in the distance.

My heart sped up and a genuine smile spread across my face for the first time in days. I slid off my stool and walked outside as casually as I could. Inside, every nerve in my body was igniting with excitement. I stood directly outside the door and waited for fourteen of my closest friends to round the corner. They had agreed to come support me in my opening. None of them would ever turn down the opportunity to get a new tattoo even though they had all seen me at least twice for one.

This group was the one Annette was concerned about and the timing couldn't have been better. As the last of them pulled up, I watched Annette walk out of the coffee shop. She took one look at them and stumbled backward, into the front of the building. She put her head down and scurried away as quickly as she could.

My absolute best friend stopped right next to me as the rest of the group filed in across the street. I barely gave Declan time to remove his helmet before wrapping my arms around him. "I am so happy to see you. These past few days..." I felt his arms tighten around me briefly before he released me.

He leaned back so he could see around me and took in the outside of my shop. His eyes widened and he grinned at me. "Dakota. I know you have a slight edge to your personality but I'm not sure this is the best way to attract potential clients."

I didn't need to look to know what he was referring to. The word 'murderer' had been etched into my mind deep enough that I didn't think it would ever go away. I could only laugh. "Is it too much? I thought it might spice up the business. You know, add a little personality to this wholesome town."

He nodded. "You're going to have to tell me that story later."

"You know I will. You're going to love it." I leaned from side to side, trying to see around Declan. "Um, are you missing someone?" As if on cue, Diesel poked his head out of the basket on the back of the bike. The sphynx cat was wearing a custom helmet with his name on the front and skull on the back that matched the emblem on his owner's vest. He meowed and pushed his head forward so he could rub his face on my hand. "Hey, little guy."

I reached into my pocket and pulled out a key, dropping it in Declan's hand. "Don't mind all the boxes, I haven't had time to unpack. The fridge and cabinets are full though, so help yourself."

"Let me know what time you'll be around. I'll make you dinner." He leaned forward and kissed me on the cheek before making his way down the road.

A small part of me hoped they would choose to take a detour around the town green. If my estimation was correct, they would be riding by just as Annette was making her way into the town hall building. Of course, my line of thinking was petty but her initial reaction to my friends, before even meeting them, and then again when she saw them was worse. I wouldn't mind if they put her a little on edge.

Chapter 7

Declan spent the night at my house while the rest of the guys stayed at the hotel. I always found it a little odd, but he preferred a night on a couch to a hotel room. I didn't mind. I would take his company any way I could get it. From the first day I met him, I found a level of comfort that I never had with anyone else.

When I woke up, I tip-toed to the kitchen so I wouldn't wake him. I glanced over and saw Diesel curled up on his chest. It warmed my heart because I knew the cat felt the same way about him as I did. I made a pot of coffee, poured myself a cup, and went out the back door to enjoy the quiet of the morning. I had just taken my first sip when I heard a soft mew. Diesel had his front paws and nose pressed against the screen in the door.

I let him out and he curled up on my lap. I would never trust my own cat to come outside, but fortunately, she never wanted to. She would barely even look out a window. Diesel loved being outside. He purred himself to sleep and stayed there until I had to move him once I finished my coffee. I set him on the kitchen table and went to take a shower.

I turned the water off and wrapped a towel around myself. I hadn't even gotten to wipe the condensation from the mirror when I heard a knock at the front door. I rolled my eyes. I really hoped this wasn't going to become a regular occurrence. I was prepared to ignore the inconvenience when I heard a second knock and something fall in the living room. I opened the bathroom door as quietly as I could and slipped down the hallway. I poked my head around the corner just enough to see Declan open the front door.

Annette gasped and stepped backward, teetering on the top step of the front porch. I couldn't say that I blamed her given her unfounded idea of bikers as a whole but I did have to stifle a laugh. For those who didn't know him, Declan could look intimidating.

He stood at 6'3" with a fully bearded face. His shoulders and biceps proved he worked out five days a week. Outside of his black, sleeveless shirt, his arms showed years of artwork depicting skulls, knives, and snakes. I'd been responsible for a number of them over the years. What Annette couldn't see from her position was the teddy bear on his shoulder in memory of his baby sister or the portrait of his niece on his thigh. She also couldn't see the color realistic quoll, displaying his favorite furry animal.

He stared at her for a moment, Diesel perched on his shoulder like a parrot. "Can I help you?" His voice matched his size, deep with a tone that told you he meant business, even when he didn't.

Annette still wore the look of shock and terror on her face. "I...I was looking for Dakota, but I can come back later."

"I think she's just out of the shower. I can go get her for you."

"No. That's okay. I'll...come back later." She stepped backwards down the front steps and hurried to her car parked at the end of the driveway.

Declan closed the door and looked at me. "I don't think she expected to see me. Friend of yours?"

"Hardly. That was Annette."

"Annette, huh? Wish I'd have known. I would have invited her in for coffee."

"And I would have thrown you into the street. There is coffee in the kitchen, though."

"You do know the way to my heart." He winked and gave me a sideways grin on his way by. "Nice towel."

"Oh, shut up."

Fiona texted me the night before, as promised. She didn't get much from the conversation between Carly and Annette, but she did provide one piece of information that was new to me; Maggie had a boyfriend. A brief internet search was all it took and I had his age, phone number, address, and employer.

There wasn't any place in town that took a long time to get to; it was only ten minutes from one side of town to the other. But Caleb was only two streets away. After getting ready for work, I left Declan on his own and headed out early so I could stop at Caleb's house on my way to the shop. It wasn't anything I had planned so I had no idea what I wanted to ask him. I would have to make it up as I went.

I parked on the street and sat in my Jeep for a few minutes, staring at his house. It was so welcoming.

Its paint was a light blue with beige shutters that matched the front door. There was a cobblestone walk to his front porch. Flowering plants lined the walkway and continued as hanging pots and flower beds on his porch. His mailbox looked like an exact replica of his cottage style home.

I cautiously made my way to his door and watched it opened as I raised my hand to knock. "Uh, hi." I could feel my face redden. I thought I would have at least a few seconds before he answered.

"Dakota. How can I help you?" It looked as if he had just woken up. He was wearing a swim team t-shirt and buffalo plaid pants. His feet were bare and he scratched his head while he yawned.

"I know this is probably a really hard time for you, but I was hoping I might be able to talk to you about Maggie." I watched as he tried to keep his face from screwing up.

"I guess, yeah." He stepped forward and pulled the door almost closed so I couldn't see inside. "What do you want to know?"

"You two were dating, right? Do you know if she was having any trouble with anyone?"

"You mean besides you?"

I sighed. "I only met her once. And I would hardly consider our interaction trouble. It was merely a misunderstanding."

"Well, she wasn't having trouble or misunderstandings with anyone else. So, if you're looking for a scapegoat, you're going to have to try someone else."

This was not going well. "If someone was accusing you of murder and you were innocent, wouldn't you do everything you could to try to clear your name?"

He shrugged. "The truth? No. Because I would never find myself in that position to begin with because I'm not a murderer." As he was finishing his sentence, the door behind him opened and a face appeared in the crack.

"Caleb? Who are you talking to?"

Carly.

After Caleb swiftly closed the door in my face, I sat in my Jeep and called detective Landry. I got another lecture about minding my own business and leaving the detective work to him. He didn't try to hide his annoyance at my telling him that Maggie had a boyfriend. He assured me he already knew about Caleb and had verified the teacher's alibi for the night someone killed her. The only recognition I received from the call was when I not so casually blurted out, "Well, did you know her boyfriend and best friend are seeing each other?"

He initially met the question with silence and then followed up with a muttered, "no."

The day was already starting to warm and the sun was shining directly into my windshield. I couldn't tell if it was the sun or the frustration building up that was making my face sweat. I put my windows down and enjoyed the breeze as I drove to the shop. I went to the coffee shop first, before going to my own, hardly able to wait to ask Fiona if she knew about Carly and Caleb. Her wide eyes and slack jaw told me she didn't.

"It doesn't surprise me. My understanding is that Carly also dated Leyland and there was a big blow up between her and Maggie when Maggie started dating him after they broke up. I know it was years ago but maybe her way of getting revenge on Maggie was to see her current boyfriend."

"Do you think that would be enough to kill someone over?" My gut was telling me 'no.' I would think the distorted pleasure would be in Maggie finding out about them, causing the same hurt she had caused Carly all those years ago. Killing her would be extreme.

"I'm probably not the best person to ask. I don't think there's ever a reason to murder someone, unless, of course, you kill in self-defense. Although, I suppose it's possible."

I couldn't help but chuckle a little. "Contrary to popular belief, I don't believe in murder, either." I thanked her for the drink and walked across the street to my shop. Sierra, Cheyenne, Willow, and Dallas were just approaching the door.

"Good morning." I slid my key in the lock and looked back at them. "Where's Riley?"

Dallas shook her head. "Your detective friend came to the hotel this morning and asked her to meet him at the station."

"Fantastic. We may need to adjust the schedule a bit this morning." I had shifted in to work mode so the artists wouldn't have to share my concerns. For days, I had been his prime suspect, although I still had no idea why, and he hadn't asked me to go to the station yet. Alex must have something he thinks is concrete evidence against Riley, otherwise she would be here with the rest of us. The one flaw in his line of thinking was that Riley wasn't even in town yet when Maggie was killed.

I scheduled all my friends periodically throughout the day with the rest of the spots filled mostly with people from out of town. I made plans to meet the guys at the diner at the end of the day. Temperance was nice enough to keep the restaurant open late again. I knew my friends were here to support me and it gave them a reason to take a road trip, but I still felt bad about not being able to spend more time with them while they were here. Of course, they all knew they didn't need an excuse. All they needed to do was send me a message letting me know they were on their way and I would welcome them every time.

Riley didn't show up to the shop until almost three hours after we opened. Whichever artist didn't have an appointment scheduled, gladly stepped up to fill in for her. She tried to apologize when she arrived, but I waved her off. It wasn't her fault and I certainly wasn't going to hold it against her.

I introduced each of my artists to my friends as they arrived and it took no time at all for the shop to fill with enough conversation that it overshadowed the music coming from the speakers. This was one of the many reasons I loved my friends; they could make conversation with any one and they made everyone around them comfortable.

By the time I got to the diner, all the guys were there waiting for me. Most already had plates of food in front of them. I was so grateful for Temperance, who smiled and waved as I walked in. For the second time in three days, she had kept the diner open late just for my friends. Throughout my life, I had come to believe diners all ran on a twenty-four hour schedule. I quickly learned that was not the case in a small town setting. Every business in town adjusted their hours according to the season and how many tourists they had. Being right on the lake, summer saw the longest hours and the most guests.

"Hey, Dakota? Are you going to finally fill us in on how you managed to make so many enemies and just as many friends in only a couple of days?" Jack was the one you could always count on to say what everyone else was thinking. He was tall and lanky. At a glance, he looked to be one of the most innocent of the group, but I had seen him get into a number of squabbles throughout the years and he was the most likely to tear someone to shreds if it came to that.

I groaned and sat on an empty stool at the counter. "Long story short? My first night here, I got into a public argument with someone and she wound up dead by the next morning. Half the town thinks I did it, the other half has my back." I didn't want to go into a lot of detail, so I kept the information to a minimum.

Clyde, who we affectionately referred to as "Grandpa" because of his age, he was fifty-four, stopped mid-bite and set his fork down. "You need us to bust some heads? 'Cus, you know we'll do it." He was an old soul who would have fit in perfectly seventy or eighty years ago.

"As much as I appreciate the offer, I have to decline your services. The thorn-in-everyone's-side-town-gossip already thinks you're all only here to cause trouble. Let's not give her a reason to feel she can justify her assumption."

The door to the diner swung open and a tall, thin blonde walked in. She stopped six inches in front of me and stared at me before pointing a long, boney finger in my face. "You need to leave my brother alone."

"Could you be a bit more specific since I don't know who you are?"

She let out a quick puff of air, clearly insulted that I didn't know her. "I'm Laura Bailey. Leyland is my brother."

"Ah, Leyland. You mean the guy who walked into my shop, the one who introduced himself to me, the man who paid me to give him a tattoo? That Leyland? Yeah, I'll do my best to tear myself away from him."

Laura rolled her eyes "There's no need to be rude."

"Rude? You're the one who just let yourself in to my reunion dinner with my friends and demanded I leave your brother alone. I've never met you before and I've only met your brother once, as a client. I'm going to recommend you take your own advice and leave so I can enjoy the rest of my evening. I'll even get the door for you." I slid off the stool and pushed the door open. The bell above chimed and seemed to echo in the nearly silent diner.

Laura huffed and stormed out, muttering under her breath.

Chapter 8

Declan and I pulled up to my house at the same time. I gathered my phone, keys, and bag and almost hit him when I opened the door. "I'm so sorry. I didn't realize you were so close."

"Doesn't matter. It looks like you had a visitor." He nodded his head toward the front window of my house.

My eyes followed his gesture to a shattered pane of glass in the picture window. "Oh. What the..."

"Give me your keys and stay behind me."

He reached his hand out and I dropped my keys into it. "You don't think they're still here, do you?"

He shook his head. "No. But I don't want to risk you going in first, just in case."

I watched as he tried the knob first, before inserting the key. He pushed the door open quietly and cautiously took a step inside. We walked through each room in the house, checking the locks on the windows and doors as we went. Nothing seemed to be out of place.

In the kitchen, we found Harley peering down at us from the top of the refrigerator. I reached up to scratch her on the head, remembering I also had a guest cat. "Diesel? Diesel?" I heard a small crash and a lower cabinet door popped open. Diesel poked his head out, looked side to side, and darted out, climbing the pant leg of Declan's jeans.

"Hey, Buddy." He plucked him off his pant leg and set him on his shoulder before going back to the living room. "Huh." He squatted down and picked up a rock wrapped in paper, bound with a rubber band. "Looks like typical television harassment." He handed the rock to me.

I sat on the couch and peeled off the rubber band. The paper wrapped around the rock was one of the flyers I had been putting up on my way here. It had been torn in half with a message written on the back in red ink.

LEAVE
BEFORE YOU MEET
THE SAME FATE AS
MAGGIE.

I looked at Declan and sighed. "Well. It looks like we've moved from harassment to threats." I handed the paper to him and watched his face grow hard as he read it.

"It looks to me like you just went from a weekend guest to a roommate until we straighten out this mess." He handed the note back to me and I could see how tense he was.

I read the message three more times hoping I might see something I hadn't noticed yet. I had no idea what I might be looking for. The letters were all a typical, capital block style with no telling characteristics. I doubted they would be able to figure out who wrote it based on the handwriting itself. I believed it was an empty threat, someone trying to scare me. I also didn't believe it would be important enough for Alex to bring in a handwriting expert or to have a paper analysis done.

"This isn't one of my flyers." I went to the desk that sat against the far wall of my living room and pulled out one of the flyers I had been posting. "It might be a little hard to tell because the one they left is all wrinkled, but it's definitely different." I handed both papers to Declan so he could compare.

He was rubbing both pages between his thumb and fingers. "Why would anyone go through the trouble of making a copy? They would have had to take down the original anyway. And I doubt they went and put it back up."

"I was wondering the same thing." I sunk into the couch, rested my head on the back, and closed my eyes. "I was so excited to come out here. Happy to have my own shop in a quiet town where I didn't have anyone else to worry about. I've been out here for five days and the only quiet I've had is my morning coffee and that's only when no one decided to knock on my door at the crack of dawn. Five days and I'm already questioning my decision."

He rested his hand on my leg. "Stop. You know you made the right decision. We talked about it, remember? This is a lot for anyone to deal with, new in town or not. We're going to call that detective of yours and have him come out to look at your window and then you're going to get some sleep to make sure the last day of your grand opening is successful. After that, you can focus your attention on this Maggie mess, okay?"

I leaned forward and wrapped my arms around him. "I'm so glad you're here. Are you really going to stay?" I was never one to rely on other people but just knowing he was here made a huge difference in how I was feeling.

"I'm not going anywhere until I know you're safe. You do have to admit, though, it's kind of funny that I'm worried about you now in this quaint town and I never thought twice about it when you were in the city."

"That's because you know I can take care of myself. But this is different. This is an entire town full of people who don't want me here. I have no idea who I can trust."

"Me." He slipped his arm around my shoulder and pulled me close to him. "You can trust me." He kissed the top of my head, knowing it always made me feel better. "Now. Call the detective."

Alex's visit to my house was pointless. He took the note as evidence but said someone making a copy of my flyer didn't mean anything. I felt better about the situation before he stopped by.

I was able to fall asleep easier, knowing Declan was only a room away, than I would have if he wasn't. I was never a fearful person, but it didn't hurt to be cautious when someone was trying to threaten me. Normally, when someone offered assistance of some kind, I turned them down. On the rare occasion I felt I needed help, I would ask. But there was something different about Declan, I had a tough time saying 'no.' I think it was the knowledge that he offered help because he genuinely cared and not because it was the right thing to do or because he felt he had to.

I slept much later than I ever did. The sunlight was already streaming through my window and the distinct aroma of coffee and bacon had made its way through my bedroom door. I padded to the kitchen in a pair of flannel pants and a tank top. "Good morning."

He greeted me with a smile. "Morning. I made coffee." He nodded to the coffee maker and went back to pushing scrambled eggs around the frying pan. He stood at the stove, shirtless and barefoot. His jeans sagged just enough to see the waistband of his boxers. A metal chain hung from a belt loop and trailed to his back pocket where faded marks indicated the worn denim from the corners of his wallet.

"Coffee? It looks like you made an entire breakfast buffet."

He shrugged. "I thought you deserved something nice."

"So, you were hungry?" I leaned around him so I could see in the pan.

"Starving." The corner of his mouth twitched up. "But I did make enough for you, too."

"Mhm. Such a gentleman." I poured us each a cup of coffee and sat at the table, watching as he scooped a miniature portion of eggs onto a small plate and added half a slice of bacon. He set it on the floor for Diesel.

He noticed me watching him and raised his eyebrows. "He was starving, too."

We talked about how I was feeling about the shop opening and what my schedule looked like for the next week. I had originally planned to use the next two days off to unpack the boxes that were creating an obstacle course in my house. Due to the last few days, my plans had changed. "I don't have anything scheduled again until Wednesday night. Even though I was going to use the next couple of days to get my life in order, I'm going to use them to go sleuthing, instead. I don't even know if Cheyenne and Riley can go home at this point. What I do know is I'm going to make sure their names and mine come off that suspect list."

"You need to be careful, Dakota. If you start sticking your nose in other people's business, you're going to make a lot of enemies."

"Half the town already doesn't like me. Besides, you know I'm not shy. I make enemies everywhere I go."

He laughed off my statement, reminding me that I don't make enemies, I simply have a knack for finding people who think my personality is intimidating. He wasn't wrong.

I showered and was getting ready for the day when my phone pinged with a text message from Cheyenne.

LOOKS LIKE I'M HERE A FEW MORE DAYS.
I'M NOT ALLOWED TO LEAVE THE STATE.

I almost dropped my phone before shooting off a quick response telling her to meet me at the shop as soon as possible.

I put all the windows down in my Jeep for the drive. It felt more like a summer morning than spring. The sun was hot on my skin and I knew the day was going to bring a much warmer temperature than the past few. I wasn't going to argue. I lived for hot, summer days and never let a day full of sunshine get away from me.

Cheyenne was standing outside as I drove past the shop, shifting from one foot to the other. It was that nervous energy again that I had come to expect from her. I parked, put my windows all the way up, and locked the doors. I didn't think it would be a requirement once I moved out here but fortunately, I had already made a habit of it from being in the city.

"Hey. Let's go sit on the bench for a few minutes." I nodded toward the bakery where a cement bench was set up facing the street. Small bushes with yellow flowers flanked both ends. They had just blossomed in the last two days. I had the same rhododendron bushes under my shop windows.

Cheyenne followed me over, walking toward the bench in a mechanical manner as if someone else were controlling her movements. She dropped onto the bench, slamming her bags into the sidewalk. She looked defeated, face drawn, bags under her bloodshot eyes. She looked at me and sighed. "I swear. I didn't know it was her, how could I? I didn't mean anything by it and I promise you, I didn't hurt her." The words tumbled out and I was having trouble keeping up.

"Slow down and start at the beginning. I'm not sure I follow."

She took a few deep breaths and her shoulders rose and fell as she decided where to begin. "So, there's this really popular blog online. It's not popular because it's good, it's popular because it's controversial. Like, as you're reading it, you just know the writer has completely lost her mind. It's obvious that it's written purposely to get a rise out of people, it's a complete train wreck, but once you read a couple posts, you have to go back every week to see what's new. You know it's going to make you mad, but you can't help it and no matter how hard you try, you're going to find a post every once in a while, that you just have to reply to.

"I've replied a few times but hadn't done so for months. And then a few weeks ago, she posted something that just stuck in my craw and I fired off a response saying someone should do us all a favor and take her out. But I didn't mean it. You know I'd never hurt anyone."

I watched, confused, as tears sprung to her eyes, her cheeks flushed. "Cheyenne, what are you talking about?"

"You know it's easy to hide behind the internet. The blogger that I'm talking about writes under the pseudonym, Veronica Tandy."

My stomach sank at hearing that name. When Leyland came into the shop, claiming he was taking Maggie's appointment, it wasn't her name that was on my schedule. It was Veronica Tandy. "Veronica was Maggie?"

Cheyenne closed her eyes and nodded, swallowing back tears.

"How did you find out?"

"Detective Landry. He stopped by this morning and read the comment I left on her blog. He asked if I had heard it before and when I told him I wrote it, he wanted to know what I meant by it. I told him it was just a rant because her post made me angry. It wasn't until after he asked me thirty other questions that he told me Veronica Tandy was really Maggie Scott."

"How did he know they were the same person?"

"He confiscated her laptop."

Taking her phone and her computer made sense. It would give him a way to piece together her timeline for the couple of days leading up to her death.

That thought brought me back to Leyland again. When he came to the shop, he had her planner with him. I wondered if Alex had been able to get his hands on it.

Chapter 9

During my breaks I started making a list of things I needed to talk to Alex about. I also wanted to follow up on some people I had already talked to him about. Most of the day was quiet until my last client. Janice Watts is the owner of the gift shop which is directly next to my shop. She talked about inheriting the business from her mother when she got sick. It made sense considering how young she was. Janice was one of those people who could talk about other people for hours and never tire of it. That's something I would normally do my best to steer away from but the information she was providing, assuming it was credible, would add a lot to my list of stops I had planned for the next two days.

It wasn't a long day as far as work, but after listening to Janice and then going to dinner with my artists to thank them for a wonderful opening, exhaustion completely took over by the time I got home. I stood in my driveway and sighed, staring at the wooden slab covering my front window. I paused when I stepped through the doorway. Reduced to a pile of broken-down cardboard, the box hazard in my living room was gone. My wall of bookcases was full, including the few knick-knacks that added a little personality to the shelves. My television was mounted to the wall above the stone fireplace and a small flicker bounced off the wall from a candle on my coffee table.

I found Declan sprawled out, socked feet on the table, head resting on the back of the couch. He had Diesel, who was no doubt soaking up his body heat, cradled in the nook of his arm. I felt a slight pull at my heart at the thought of him spending the day getting my house in order without me asking just because he knew how much better it would make me feel.

I dropped my bag and keys on the table and walked over to the bookshelves to admire his work. Each shelf was full and every corner had one book with the cover facing forward. I heard a small rustle behind me.

"Don't worry. They're all alphabetized by last name. Except the signed copies, they're all in front."

I turned to see his sideways grin, telling me he was proud of his accomplishment while simultaneously making fun of my obsessive quality about my book collection. His grin made me smile; it always did. It was a gesture reserved for those he was closest to, people he was comfortable enough with to let his guard down. "What did I do to deserve this?"

"Nothing. I just thought you'd appreciate it. It might not be perfect, but at least I cleaned up the boxes." He shrugged and shifted Diesel to his lap, tapping the couch cushion beside him. "Want to finish watching the movie with me?"

Smokin' Aces. Declan would watch the movie every day if he could. I sat down next to him and curled my legs up beside me. "You do know I love a little Ray Liotta in my life. And you're right. I very much appreciate you doing this for me. I can cross this off my list along with some of the tension I've been feeling."

"I need to give you a lot of credit. You've had a really long week and I don't know that I could keep it together as well as you have been."

"Don't let me fool you. I'm only keeping it together on the outside, it's a complete facade. I have a list a mile long of stuff I need to do. I feel awful about spending almost no time with my artists, I've barely got to see the guys while they were here. I feel like my brain may actually explode."

"I've got good news, it won't. It's a good thing, too, because I don't mind emptying boxes, but I don't want to clean that up. And, as far as the guys are concerned, they were here to support you. They knew it wasn't a social visit. It was a beautiful ride down here and none of them are arguing being able to spend an entire weekend on their bikes."

"Still, I wish I would have planned better."

"They all know how to find you. As far as your artists, maybe you can plan another event for next summer when all the tourists are here and you can invite them back again."

I stared at the television, thinking about what he said. It probably wasn't a bad idea. If I started planning soon, I could host an event during the busiest week of tourist season.

"Hey." Declan swatted my leg with the back of his hand to get my attention. "You good?"

"Yeah, sorry. I was just thinking about what you said. It's a great idea. Well, as long as the artists are willing to come back after what has happened this time."

"They'll be fine and I'm glad I could help. Where are we heading first tomorrow?"

"We?" The word came out as a mix of shock and snark. I wasn't planning to have anyone tag along. I never considered the possibility because I always did everything myself.

He let out a quick puff of air. "You don't think I'm going to let you go by yourself? There's a killer out there and half the town thinks it's you. I don't need to insert myself into your sleuthing but I'm going to be there in case you get into trouble."

I sighed and nodded my head once. There would be no point in arguing with him. He was as stubborn as they come and I knew he already had his mind made up. "I'm going to see Annette first." I watched as he creased his brow. "I'll be nice. I'm sure she probably means well in her own, weird way, but I can't help feeling like there's something she's not saying, some reason she's so invested in this."

I didn't leave my house until just after eight. Unlike the rest of the town, I found it rude to go knocking on people's doors so early. It worked out well because since I was going to see Annette first, I could meet her at the town hall. It wasn't ideal since it's the first place we met and it wasn't the best introduction, but it was as close to neutral territory as we could get.

I always found government buildings cold and unwelcoming. No matter how hard they tried to spruce them up, there was always a cloud, showering depression over the structure. The employees had to feel it as well since they all had the same, dull personality. None of them ever seemed happy.

I left Declan in the Jeep and entered the building through the same door I had used almost exactly a week ago. Last week, I walked in hopeful and ready to introduce myself to everyone. Today, I had a chip on my shoulder, but I was trying hard to shake it off.

The building hadn't been renovated since it was built and it showed. Directly inside the door, a bulletin board with room names and numbers hung on the wall and arrows indicated which direction a person should go to find certain rooms. With no one there to greet you, it leaned further toward the side of unwelcoming.

I stood outside Annette's door and took a deep breath before plastering on a friendly smile. I pulled the door open and Annette swung around wearing the same fake smile I did.

"Good mor...oh, it's you." Her voice went from one of a cheery welcome, albeit fake, to one of disdain.

"Good morning. I'm sure you're probably busy but I was hoping we might be able to talk for a few minutes."

"Why? So you can proclaim your innocence? Let me save you the trouble. No matter what you say, it won't change my mind. The sooner Detective Landry can build a case against you, the better." She grabbed a stack of files from a desk behind the counter and turned her back toward me.

I watched her for a moment, her jerky motions opening the filing cabinet drawers, stuffing folders in where it was already about to burst. "I understand your reluctance to outsiders, I get the bias you have against tattoos and the kind of people who get them. I grew up in a very conservative household with both my parents thinking the exact same way. I thought for sure when I got my first tattoo I would break their hearts. I thought they would shatter when I told them I wanted to be an artist. But, they met my friends, they saw my work, and they came around. I hope, in time, you'll be able to as well."

She slammed the second stack of files back on the desk and glared at me. "Let me be perfectly clear with you, Dakota. I don't want you here. I don't care about you or your little, probably made up, heartwarming story. What I care about is feeling safe in my own community. I care about the safety of my family. I care about having to attend my niece's funeral because someone murdered her."

My breath caught in my throat and I needed a moment to process what she just said. The only part of Annette that moved was her face as it went from anger to shock. She hadn't meant for that piece of information to come out. "Maggie is your niece?"

She picked up the stack of files and turned her back to me again. "I think you need to leave."

The day had brightened significantly in the short amount of time I was inside. The cloud cover disappeared and the air had started to warm. Declan was leaning against my Jeep, his arms crossed. Diesel sprawled on the roof, soaking in the sun's rays.

I slid into the passenger seat without a word. Declan had offered to be my chauffeur for the day and I didn't argue with him. As much as I loved driving, I hated having passengers in my car. He set Diesel on my lap and started the engine. "So, I'm guessing you need coffee?"

"Is it that obvious or do you just know me that well?"

"Both."

I did have plans to go to the coffee shop to talk to Fiona anyway, but I didn't see her when I walked in. My heart sank when I saw Carly running the register. I wasn't looking to converse with her today. For the second time this morning, I put on my best friendly smile and approached the counter. I watched Carly spin around, trying to find anyone that would be able to take over for her, but she was stuck. I heard her sigh before she turned around and delivered her version of a smile.

"How can I help you?" Her voice was unnaturally high. It was the customer service voice that one might use when they were trying to be friendly because they were at work, but everyone knew it wasn't real.

I ordered my coffee and watched her face contort as she rung it up. "And I need a large dark roast with a splash of milk." I waited for her to finish our drinks, keeping my fingers crossed that no one came in behind me. It was the quietest I had seen the shop since I'd arrived in town. I noticed they changed their advertisement on the chalkboard to reflect a new flavor of iced tea. Pomegranate. *Gross.*

Carly set my coffee on the counter next to Declan's with more force than was necessary and turned her back to me.

"Carly? Can we talk for a minute?"

"I'm busy."

"Please?"

She hesitated before turning to face me. "If you're looking for an apology for me going to talk to Alex, you're not going to get one. I admit I may have been wrong about the reason you were at the center, but you're a suspect in a murder. You can't blame me for wanting to feel safe." She picked up a cloth and started wiping down the counters.

"I don't blame you. Just like you shouldn't blame me for wanting to find the real killer. I just have a couple of questions and then I promise I'll leave you alone."

She rolled her eyes and sighed. "Fine."

"Thank you. You two were best friends, did she tell you she was writing a blog under a different name?"

"No. We didn't tell each other everything." The look on her face told me a different story. It told me she did know but I wasn't supposed to.

"Okay. Do you have any idea why no one has mentioned that Annette is her aunt?"

She stopped wiping the counter and squinted her eyes. "What are you talking about? See, this is why you shouldn't be snooping around. Where did you come up with that idea?"

"Annette." I didn't offer any additional information.

Carly went back to wiping the already cleaned counters. "Yeah, well. She probably told you that to get rid of you. Besides, you can't really believe anything she says, she makes stuff up as she goes."

"That's useful information to have. I'll keep that in mind." A silence hung in the air between us while I struggled with whether or not to ask my next question.

"Are we done here?" I really do have work to do."

Now or never. "Almost. Um, did Maggie know you were also seeing her boyfriend?" The bell on the door chimed indicating a customer entering and Carly walked away from me with no response to my question.

It was only mid-morning but my stomach rumbled as I walked across the street to my shop. I had let Declan in to view the security footage from the night before. Diesel curled in a ball outside the door. He watched me cross the street through squinted eyes, annoyed that we wouldn't allow him inside. "Just a couple more minutes." I made a few kissy noises at him before going inside. "Find anything good?"

Declan took his coffee from my hand and took a sip before answering. "A whole lot of absolutely nothing. Once it gets dark, it's like a ghost town out here. So different from city life." He set his coffee on the counter and gazed at me. "So different. Are you sure you're going to be happy here?" He didn't ask the question maliciously, although it was the opposite of how he was speaking to me last night, his question held a genuine concern.

"I will be incredibly happy. You know, once I'm no longer a murder suspect."

Chapter 10

We drank our coffee while scrolling through the rest of the security footage. Finding nothing more than two cars passing by and a curious raccoon trying to claw its way through the back door, we both sat back and relaxed for a moment.

I wanted to visit the library to look through some archives. If I had any hope of finding information about Annette and her family, that would be the best place to find it. Knowing it may take a few hours, Declan and I drove back to my house for an early lunch.

In all the years I had known Declan, I had cooked for him exactly twice. Those two experiences led to my banishment to my own back porch after collecting some glasses and a pitcher of iced tea. He didn't even trust me enough to make sandwiches. He slid a plate containing a single layer sandwich in front of me. The one he placed in front of himself was reminiscent of one from the old Blondie and Dagwood comics. The only thing it was missing was the toothpick with an olive stabbed onto it. He had just taken his first over-exaggerated bite with we heard a knock at the front door.

"I'll get it. Don't worry, I'm better at answering the door than doing anything in the kitchen." I heard his stilted laugh as the door closed behind me.

I pulled open the front door to find the sweetest looking woman. Her gray hair formed a perfect bun on the top of her head. She wore a flowered dress and round, oversized glasses. A pearl bracelet adorned her wrist and the smallest button nose gave her a youthful appearance despite the wrinkles on her face. "Hi. Can I help you?"

Her smile made her face scrunch up. I'm Mitzi. I do hope I'm not being a burden, but I wanted to introduce myself and I think I may have some information that you would find helpful."

"It's nice to meet you. I'm sure you know I'm Dakota. Why don't you come in? We just sat down in back." I opened the door wider to welcome her in. I stopped in the kitchen to collect another glass from the cabinet and lead her to the porch. "Please, have a seat. This is my friend, Declan. This is Mitzi."

"Well, I don't remember seeing you on the lunch menu."

Declan's cheeks turned a light shade of pink and I had to fight off a smile.

She took the seat next to him and I imagined her feet barely reaching the ground. She reached out and grabbed Declan's bicep. "Mhm. You'd be in trouble if I was twenty years younger."

Declan nearly choked on his drink. "Twenty?"

"Oh, maybe closer to fifty, but a girl can dream."

I watched his eyes widen and as much as I wanted to see his full reaction, I needed to move our meeting along so we could still get over to the library.

"So, Mitzi? You said you had some information we might find helpful?"

She released Declan's arm like she just realized she was still holding it. "Yes. I wanted to tell you first not to worry about Annette. She may be rude and she may buy her knickers pre-bunched, but she's harmless; just likes to hear herself talk. Anyway, what I think you'll be interested in..."

Diesel jumped up from his spot on his chair, fast enough to make it rock back and forth, swatting at a bug flying over his head.

Mitzi jumped back, gasped, and threw her hand over her heart. "What in the wrinkled spawn of Satan is that thing?"

Declan stood and gathered the cat in his arms. "This is my cat, Diesel."

"He's naked. And you should tell him, unlike him, I only have one life and he almost just ended it."

Declan laughed. "I'm sorry he scared you."

"I'm sorry he looks like that." She gave a fake shudder and scrunched her face. "I've eaten prunes with less wrinkles than that thing." She narrowed her eyes and looked directly at Diesel when she spoke, clearly trying to insult him. "Anyway, what I wanted to tell you is that you should be looking at Caleb, Maggie's boyfriend. He's a teacher here in town. Although, I'm not sure why anyone would trust him around their children."

"What makes you say that?" I didn't tell her we had already spoken to him. Or tried to speak to him. I would take any information she had to offer.

"Well, to start, he's extremely hot tempered, always has been. I also heard him and Maggie fighting a few days before her murder."

"Fighting? Where? Did you hear what they were fighting about?" This was the type of information I was hoping to hear.

"I live right next door to him. I could only hear bits and pieces of what they were saying but I did hear him say he would have no problem getting rid of her if she didn't take it down. I have no idea what he was talking about, but I think most people would say 'breaking up with' and not 'getting rid of you.' Of course, I'm old and I never know what you kids are talking about these days."

"I think I know what it was about. Did you ever see any other females going over to his house?"

"Only Carly. She's been going there for about a month now."

I could see the wheels turning in her head, the realization that Caleb was entertaining two women. "Do you know for sure he was arguing with Maggie and not Carly?"

She nodded. "Yes, dear. Her car was in the driveway."

"Have you talked to Detective Landry about what you heard?"

"Oh, no. I figure if he has questions, he'll come find me. I don't leave my house much so I'm easy to find."

Diesel curled up in Declan's lap, quietly purring from the fingers scratching behind his ears. "Mitzi, I think you should go talk to the detective. He may not know to come find you if no one told him about the argument."

"Well, handsome and smart." Mitzi looked at me and winked. "You should hang on to this one."

"We're not dating." We both replied in unison and a huge smile spread across Mitzi's face.

"It sounds like maybe you should be. But I suppose Mr. Declan is right. I should contact Detective Landry to tell him what I heard. Maybe I should tell him about Andrew, too, just in case." She stood without elaborating.

I couldn't let her leave on a comment like that. "Wait. What about him?"

"I spoke to him a few weeks ago. He's Maggie and Carly's swim coach. He was telling me there had been a falling out between the two of them. Apparently, they were both eyeing the top spot in their upcoming competition. Oh, dear, they were, anyway. I guess it's Carly's spot now." She rested her hand on Declan's shoulder. "You should get that cat some Rogaine. It was nice meeting you both. Thank you for the tea."

I walked her out and made my way back to the porch, feeling the need to inhale the sandwich I hadn't gotten to take a bite of yet. As I neared the table, I saw Diesel lying on the chair Mitzi had occupied, chewing on the corner of a piece of paper. I wrestled it out of his paws and turned it over. It was a photograph of the front of my shop. A hooded figure stood facing the building and the letters M, U, R, D had already been spraypainted on the brick. I slid the photo onto the table in front of Declan. "It looks like your friend, Mitzi, has a few secrets."

Before heading to the library, I looked up Andrew's address and decided to stop by his house first. I hadn't heard they had re-opened the rec center yet. Andrew lived on the road directly behind my shop. From his front step he would have a view of the fence that concealed the back alley of my shop, the diner, gift shop, bookstore, and bakery.

We took the long way around and drove by the rec center first. The parking lot was empty and police tape still stretched around the entrances. Andrew's road was short with only enough room for four houses with moderate spacing between them. Flower arrangements and bouquets covered the lawn next to his. Declan slowed as he neared Andrew's house but continued down the road so he could turn around. He stopped just past the flowered lawn. "Did you know Maggie lived right next to your shop?"

I could feel my mouth hanging open as I strained to look at the yard behind me. "I had no idea. I've never been over here. The farthest I've gone is out my back door, into the alley, but it's fenced off so I can't see over it." I gestured to the wooden fence on the other side of the road.

Andrew met us on his front porch when we were half-way up his driveway. "I knew you would find your way here eventually." He sat down on an old, wooden chair. I couldn't help but notice the marks on the wood porch where years on the chair legs scrapping against it had dulled the appearance. If I had to guess, I would say Andrew was in his mid-forties, nowhere near retirement age as I assumed he would be. He looked fit, no doubt due to the time spent at the rec center. "I didn't expect you to show up with a bodyguard."

"Oh, no, he's not..." I ended my sentence when I saw the look of amusement on his face and followed to where his eyes were looking. "That's Diesel. And the human is my friend, Declan. Is it okay if we ask you a few questions?"

He gestured to the chairs on the opposite side of the door for us to sit. "I actually expected you much sooner, but then I remembered you had the opening for your little shop."

My body instantly went rigid and Declan rested his hand on my knee. He knew I took issue with people belittling my line of work. "Yes, my *little* business that has me booked out months in advance has kept me busy these past few days." Declan's fingers tightened around my leg and I changed the subject. "I'm sure it's no surprise to you that I'm a suspect in Maggie's murder. I'd like to clear my name as soon as possible so I'm looking for any information that can help me do that."

Andrew nodded his head. "I would do the same if I were in your position, of course, I wouldn't ever *be* in your position..."

"Never? Because I heard you were having trouble with both Carly and Maggie." It was a question and a statement that I left hanging in the air.

"Those two had a problem with each other. They competed for everything."

Diesel jumped from Declan's shoulder to his lap before landing with a thump on the porch, racing down the steps, and rounding the side of the house.

"Best friends and competitors? How did you deal with that as their coach?"

"I didn't. I told them a long time ago I didn't care about the drama between them. When they showed up at the pool, they only had to worry about proving themselves to me. If they brought their personal lives in, I could cut them out."

"Sounds fair." It came out with more than a hint of patronization.

"They respected me. That's all that mattered."

I rolled my eyes, finding that hard to believe. "Aside from swimming, what else did they compete over?"

"I never asked. Always wondered how they could consider themselves friends, though. I never saw them getting along." He shrugged his shoulders noting it didn't matter to him either way.

I side-eyed Declan and he shook his head, barely visibly. I turned back to Andrew. "What about you? Did you get along with them?"

"They're my swimmers. They show up, they work, they go home. I'm not there to make friends." He shifted his body away from us and I knew he was growing tired of the conversation.

"I just have one more question. Did you know about Maggie's blog?"

His eyebrows raised and his lips pursed. "Do I look like the type of person to sit at home and read blogs?"

We thanked him for his time and made our way down his driveway. "Why didn't you ask him any questions?"

He shrugged. "If he wanted us to know, he would have told us."

"That's not really how an investigation works."

"I still think you should be leaving the investigating up to Alex, but since I know you won't, I'm just here to make sure you stay safe. Besides, it looks like Diesel got us all the information we probably need."

Diesel huddled behind the front tire, chomping on a balled-up piece of paper.

I opened the passenger door and he jumped in, dropping the paper in the cup holder.

Declan slid into the driver's seat and looked at me. "If you want my opinion, I don't think he hurt Maggie. But, he may be a murderer."

"What makes you say that?"

"Who owns a non-rocking porch chair?"

Chapter 11

We pulled into the parking lot of the library with reggae music blasting from the speakers. The music was Declan's guilty pleasure. It wasn't a far drive between Andrew's house and the library, but I had forgotten about the paper until Diesel dropped the ball in my lap. I straightened it as much as I could.

"Huh. Didn't Andrew say he didn't know about Maggie's blog?"

Declan nodded. "Yeah. What have you got?"

I handed him the paper; thankful Diesel only poked a few holes in it with his teeth.

"Interesting. Do you think it's him she was talking about in this one?"

"I can't say for sure, but it makes sense. It would also explain why he chose to print this one. Maybe he went to confront her and things got out of hand."

"It's possible, but my gut is still telling me he didn't do it. Let's go inside and find out what we can about Annette."

A wave of nostalgia washed over me when I opened the library's front door. Every year my mom used to bring me here at the beginning of our vacation so I could check out some books to read. I always found this library to hold a particular comfort. Made up of three floors, each contained large, plush chairs, workstations, study tables, and full-length windows on three sides.

I headed straight to the third floor where I knew they would have exactly what I was looking for. It was an extremely outdated technology but that was small town life, always years behind the rest of society.

A woman named Kerry stood behind the reference desk. She looked exactly like the last person you would expect to be a librarian. She was older than she appeared from far away. Her hair was short and spiky and her clothing style screamed bohemian. Gold and silver bangles adorned her wrists and she wore a long, tribal patterned wrap skirt and a silk scarf covered her neck.

"Hi. I'm hoping you can help me."

A large grin swept across her face. "Sure. How can I help?"

"Um. I'm looking for some birth and property records. And I'm hoping I may be able to find some marriage records as well."

"You're in the right place. What year are you looking for?"

Year? I hadn't given it that much thought. Like the rest of society, the simplicity of a Google search had spoiled me. I thought back to what I knew about Maggie and her approximate age and gave a range of five years.

"Huh. You're the second person in as many weeks to ask for that same information." She waved her hand forward and Declan and I followed her to a worktable stuffed in a corner with two over-sized, green powder-coated machines on it.

"The second? I don't suppose you can tell me who the other person was?"

Kerry gave me a sympathetic look. "While we don't exactly have a librarian-patron confidentiality agreement, we do try to extend a professional courtesy to our patrons to protect their privacy."

I bit the inside of my cheek to keep from screwing up my face. I didn't expect much but the tone in her voice told me she wouldn't budge on that policy. "I understand."

Kerry set us up on the machines and we each collected one year's worth of film. After thirty minutes, we both sat back, disgusted. "I forgot how much strain these lenses and lights put on your eyes. Micro-fiche needs to go away, for good."

We were making our way through our second years when I found what I was looking for. "I've got it." I busied myself printing all the pages I thought I needed and was so engaged with what I was doing, I didn't notice Declan had cleaned up his area and walked away.

Print outs in hand, I walked back to the reference desk where I found Declan, no doubt charming his way into getting information from Kerry. It was a skill he had acquired over the years; one I'd never quite figured out. He had an aura around him that made people open up to him and confide their deepest secrets. Most times, he didn't try, people just trusted him. Other times, like now, he could use it to his advantage.

Kerry stopped speaking to Declan as soon as she saw me. "Did you find what you were looking for?"

"I did, thank you. I may have to come back to follow-up on what I found."

"For sure. Let me know if I can assist with anything else."

I didn't miss the wink she threw Declan's way as we were turning to leave. When we got to the parking lot, I had to ask him about it. "What was that little wink all about?"

He flashed one of his crooked smiles. "My powers of persuasion won again."

"So, you flirted with her?" He knew I was teasing him. He didn't have to flirt to get what he wanted.

"Ooh, yeah. I don't think her wife would like that very much. I did find out who else was there looking for information, though. And she directed me to go chat with her wife. She thinks she may be able to help."

We drove back to my house and found Alex waiting in my driveway. It should have surprised me, but it didn't. It had been too long since I saw him, too long since he had questioned me or one of my friends because he had nothing else to go on. I was hoping for more time so I would have more concrete information to present to him before he appeared again. My plan was to look at Maggie's blog to see how far she had gotten in her mission to out as many people in her life as she could. If the post we found at Andrew's house was any indication, we could expect a lengthy list of suspects that didn't include any of my friends.

"Detective? What do we owe the pleasure?"

"The usual. Just checking in to make sure you and your friends aren't getting into any more trouble."

"Hmm. We haven't actually been in any yet. Except, of course, the things you're trying to pin on us."

"Yeah, well, we'll see about that. I sent Cheyenne home, by the way. She's not allowed to contact you until this is all over. I expect you'll do the same." He said it like a question, but I knew it wasn't. "I heard you went to visit Andrew." He left his statement open, waiting for one of us to offer the rest.

"We did."

He stared at us with irritation painted on his face. "Would you like to elaborate?"

"How do you know we went to talk to him?"

"Because I went to see him and he told me you two stopped by. He's under the impression you're trying to clear your name by pinning the murder on someone else."

I couldn't help but laugh. "Pin it on someone? No. Find the real murderer? Yes. And why wouldn't I? It's the best way I can think of to prove I didn't do it."

"So? Did you find the real killer?" His tone was condescending and accusatory.

"No." It was always a good indication that Declan was getting angry when he answered with only one or two words.

Alex snorted. "Maybe it's because she's standing right next to you."

I was looking at Alex but felt the chill around me from Declan tensing up. I took a step forward and to the side, standing between the two men. I didn't expect to be able to do anything but that was my way of telling Declan to hold it together, much like when he placed his hand on my leg earlier. "We don't have a definite answer, but we did find a few interesting facts that may get us a couple steps closer."

"Would you like to share what you found?"

"Will it make you leave my driveway?"

Alex smiled. "Last I checked, you don't live here. But, if it's useful information, it'll give me somewhere to go and I'll leave you and your girlfriend alone, for now."

My snarky attitude got the best of me before I reeled it back in. "I guess it's a good thing we didn't leave the investigating up to you." We showed him the picture Mitzi left behind and told him what we knew about Andrew.

Declan planned ahead and took a picture on his phone of both the photo and the printout Diesel pulled from Andrew's trash. Alex collected the paper and photo from us and left. I didn't tell him about the articles I printed at the library, so I still had evidence, or at least theories, to share with him later.

It wasn't until after Alex left that Declan told me where the photo from Mitzi actually came from. She didn't purposely leave it behind for us to find. Diesel helped himself to items in her wicker purse when she set it on the ground. I wasn't sure whether to be thankful or embarrassed that the cat was a thief. One thing I was sure of was it was nearly impossible to be mad at him when he looked so innocent licking his paw and using it to clean the backs of his ears.

He mewled and butted his head against my leg. I guess he also knew his cuteness overpowered any amount of anger I felt toward him.

*****

The paper we got from Andrew's proved to be beneficial in finding Maggie's blog. It had the web address printed on the bottom of the page. Declan and I spent almost three hours combing through her posts and printing out any we thought might contain important clues. We went back three years and had a healthy stack of paper by the time we finished.

"I'm going to make dinner. I'm starving." Declan raised his eyebrows at me as I stood up. He looked concerned. A small chuckle escaped my lips. "I'm making pasta. It's nearly impossible to mess up."

"Okay. Let me know if you need help boiling the water."

I rolled my eyes. "Rude." I couldn't help but smirk as I walked away. I pulled pans from the cabinets, wondering if we were any closer to figuring out the mystery.

Declan called out from the living room. "Do you have any highlighters?"

"Yeah. They should be in the top drawer of the desk." Between visitors, sleuthing, and tattooing, I had managed to get some boxes unpacked over the past few days and organizing my desk always had a top spot on my list any time I moved. I didn't question what Declan was doing. He knew what to look for. I pulled a box of frozen garlic bread slices from the freezer and placed them on a baking tray. Declan would have laughed and made fun of me if he saw me doing it. He loved to cook and made almost everything from scratch. The extent of my culinary ability was opening a box and throwing it in the oven.

I poked my head around the corner to tell him to take a break and eat. "Whoa." He had gone through the entire stack of paper and had five piles, all highlighted with assorted colors, spread over the coffee table. "Did you have any luck?"

"That depends on what you consider luck. I thought we only had three suspects. It turns out, we have five and I have no idea who suspects four and five are." He leaned back and stretched his arms behind his head. "Maybe you'll know who she's talking about?"

"I'll look in a little bit. Let's eat first."

We were enjoying a quiet meal together until we heard the shuffling of paper coming from the other room. "Diesel, get off the table." His voice was loud and deep. If I didn't know him as well as I do, I could understand how people would find him intimidating. A few minutes later, we heard the rustling again. "Diesel. Get down." We heard a thump as his paws hit the floor. He ran into the dining room, meowed, jumped on the table, and stole a piece of garlic bread.

Declan shook his head. "He was already in trouble; he might as well make it worth his time."

"How cute. He takes after you."

We cleaned up from dinner together after Declan lost the argument about it being his turn. I wanted to get it done as soon as possible so he could explain his research method to me. I put on a pot of coffee so it would be ready for dessert and we went back to the paperwork while it was brewing.

We found Diesel curled up on a few pages he had knocked to the floor. Pages now littered the surface of the table haphazardly, instead of standing in neat piles as Declan had arranged them. A sigh came from deep in his throat. "At least I was smart enough to color code them."

While he began reorganizing them into piles, I glanced at the pages Diesel was now lying belly-up on and took in the highlighted passages. One blue, one green, and two orange. From the time he was a kitten, Diesel seemed to have some sort of sixth sense. Maybe the garlic bread wasn't about trouble, maybe it was his reward for his detective-like prowess.

Chapter 12

The next morning came way too early. I threw my hair in a loose ponytail and wore a t-shirt and flannel pants. I did my best to stay quiet as I made my way to the kitchen.

Declan sprawled across the couch, one leg flung over the back, the other hanging down to the floor. His body position was a perfect representation of an over-dramatic actor in a shooting scene. The temptation to check his pulse, just in case, was there, but I didn't want to wake him.

I made a single cup of coffee and added a bit of milk to cool it down. I reached over to pet Diesel who was laying on the windowsill that he didn't fit on. He nudged his head forward and I complied with his request to scratch behind his ears. "What do you think? Should we go sit outside while we're waiting for your daddy to wake up?" Diesel meowed and jumped to the floor. "Maybe you can tell me why you pulled out those particular pages?" He looked back, stretched his front legs, and yawned. "I'll take that as a 'no'."

I opened the door and Diesel darted out in front of me, sniffing around the edge of the porch. It was still dark outside and I couldn't see where he disappeared to. A rainstorm had come through at some point overnight. Petrichor was heavy in the air and the dampness made my skin clammy. Remaining water drops soaked into my pants when I sat down. I heard a low rumble, building in volume, coming from near the porch stairs. I sat straight up, trying to adjust my vision to the darkness.

I heard a twig snap in the distance. Diesel let out a vicious yowl before racing down the steps. I heard his feet hit the steps on the way down but couldn't see which direction he went. I stood, moved closer to the stairs, and peered out. It was hard to be sure, but I thought I could just make out a human form running across the dirt road that cut between my yard and the lake. I didn't know what to do, I stood motionless, staring at the spot between the trees that bordered my property. I should give chase like Diesel was doing. I should go wake Declan up. I stood, frozen, at the top of the stairs, unable to make a decision.

The moisture and chill in the air seeped through my skin and I shivered. I looked at the ground and let out a yelp. A pair of bright, glowing eyes were staring up at me. My muscles weakened and my heart pounded. It took a moment for me to realize Diesel had returned to the deck. I started to squat down, Diesel mewed, and a flash of light burst from behind me. I jumped and spun around; my hand flew up to my chest as I yelped for the second time in less than a minute.

Declan wrapped his arms around me and pulled me toward his bare chest. "You scared me half to death. What are you doing out here?"

I erupted into a fit of nervous laughter and tears prickled my eyes. "All I was trying to do was drink a cup of coffee and enjoy the silence of the morning."

He pushed me back so he could see my face. "I think you ruined the silent morning for half the neighborhood." He flashed a crooked grin so I knew he was joking. "Are you okay? What happened?"

I felt comforted by the weight of his hands gripping my upper arms. "I'm okay. I usually come out every morning to enjoy my coffee. But Diesel started growling. He ran off toward the lake and I thought I saw a person running over by the street. I yelled because Diesel came back but I could only see his eyes glistening and I didn't know it was him. And then you scared me again when you turned on the light." The nervous laughter bubbled up again. "And I just realized how ridiculous that sounds saying it out loud." I looked into his eyes and tried to smile but there was a certain comfort in his presence where I knew I could be vulnerable.

"It doesn't sound ridiculous at all. You were out here by yourself while someone was creeping around your yard in the dark." Diesel let out a half-meow, half-growl and we both laughed. "And you did a great job protecting her."

Declan made himself coffee and came back outside to join me. We sat quietly, watching the sun rise over the lake. It was a wonderful experience being able to enjoy nature with someone I care deeply for, without feeling the need to fill the silence.

Once we were both showered and ready to go, we decided I would talk to a few people in town while Declan and Diesel rode to the city to pick up yet another security camera, this one for my house. I still couldn't believe, after living in the city for so many years, never needing extra security, I found the need for it at both my shop and my home here. It felt backwards.

I walked Declan out and he secured Diesel's helmet before leaning down to kiss my forehead. "You think you can manage to stay out of trouble for a couple hours?"

"I...will try. But no promises." He glanced at me from the corner of his eye and I laughed. "I'll stay out of trouble. You act like this is the first time I've ever gone anywhere myself."

He looked straight at me, holding his own helmet above his head, with his eyebrows raised. "Should I remind you of the time you tried to drink your coffee and enjoy the quiet of the morning on your own back porch? Because that was about two hours ago."

All through my teenage years and well into my twenties, my mother always told me I could stay home and get into trouble. She was right. No matter what I did, trouble always had a way of finding me. "On that note, I'm going to go. Enjoy your ride." I threw my bag in the seat next to me. I hated that I couldn't argue with him.

As usual, my first stop was the coffee shop. It had to be nearing capacity with the amount of people packed inside. After standing in line for nearly fifteen minutes, I barely got to say 'hello' to Fiona. Fortunately, I didn't have to speak to her for any particular reason.

I grabbed my coffee from the counter when the barista called my name and managed to find a small table with a single chair tucked in the corner. Before we left, Declan had taken pictures of all the highlighted articles and all the notes we made and I stuffed the physical copies in a folder and brought them with me. I wanted a chance to look over them one more time to make sure I had appropriate questions and to double-check that I hadn't missed any obvious clues.

At my shop, I worked alone or with two or three other people. I could adjust the volume on the radio or turn it off if I wanted to. The noise level in the coffee shop this morning was overwhelming. The music from the overhead speakers wasn't loud but added to the voices around me. I managed to read through the pages for my first visit to the realtor but couldn't concentrate any longer. I packed up my things and headed out, waving to Fiona when I passed her.

Instead of going back to the library to look up more property records, I decided it would be more beneficial to stop by to see the real estate agent, Celeste Valentine. Celeste had helped me a few months ago with purchasing my home and leasing my shop space. That was one benefit to being in a small town; without options, much of what you had to do was a one-stop shop.

Celeste and I had a good rapport so I didn't think she would mind answering a few questions for me. The agency was on the same side of the road as the coffee shop but at the far end, closer to the town green. It wasn't part of the strip the other shops occupied, it sat by itself with a lawn in front. Red and white striped awnings hung over the windows and door. Pink rhododendron bushes ran along the front of the building giving it a welcoming vibe.

She was busy typing on her computer but looked up when she heard the door open. "Dakota. I didn't think I would see you back so soon. Is everything at the shop okay?" She looked concerned and I imagined the only time she saw people after they signed a mortgage or lease was either to renew a lease or file a maintenance request.

"Oh, yes. Everything is just fine. I actually have a few questions I was hoping you could answer for me."

The main room was small with much of its space taken up by the executive, mahogany desk she was sitting behind. An old leather couch sat under one window and a water cooler and small end table stood in front of the other. The room felt dry and stale, not at all mimicking the welcome appearance from the outside.

"Sure. I'll do my best." She gestured to the chair opposite her.

"Laura and Leyland Bailey? Who owns the property they live on?" I didn't feel the need to add any niceties, so I got straight to the questions. I watched her face go from a look of enthusiasm to one of confusion.

"Leyland bought his own house last month. I think he just moved in a couple of days ago. Laura lives in her childhood home."

I knew that information already, but I felt better having her verify. "Did Leyland buy his house in his own name?"

She nodded. "Yes. He bought it outright, didn't even apply for a mortgage."

"And Laura?"

"I'll have to look into that. How soon do you need to know?"

I stared at her without uttering a word.

"I'll look into it now." She focused her brown eyes on the computer screen while her perfectly manicured fingers pecked at the keyboard and mouse button.

I stared at the top of her head while she worked. Shiny strands of gray were beginning to emerge from her part line in her otherwise flawless, curly hair. Lost in thought, I wondered if she would be able to give me the information I needed.

"Here we go. It was a number of years ago, so I wanted to double-check my memory. Her parents owned the house and transferred it to Laura. All she has to do is pay the taxes on it."

"Are they up to date?"

"I don't have that information. You'd have to go to the town hall and talk to Annette." Her voice trailed off and she looked into my eyes. "Sorry. I've heard you two don't exactly have the best relationship."

"We don't. But that's okay. Maybe I'll have my friend, Declan, talk to her." I smiled at the thought of how I imagined that interaction would go.

"Oh." I watched as her eyes lit up and a smile crossed her face. "I saw him the other day." She put her head down and raised her eyes, sheepishly, toward me. "Are you two...?"

I chuckled. "No. But you'd have to fight Mitzi for him."

"In that case, I don't stand a chance."

I smiled at her as I stood to leave. "Thank you for all your help. I really appreciate it."

I went to the shop to write down what I knew so far. Even with the sun coming through the front windows, I immediately noticed the light in the storage room was on. I turned my head as an automatic response to listen for any indication that someone was still there. I tried to think back to the previous day when Declan and I stopped. *Did either of us go back there?*

I took my phone from my pocket and sent him a message. I had barely hit the send button when his face popped up on my screen.

I didn't get a chance to say hello before his voice came through. "What's going on?" He sounded distraught.

"Nothing. I was curious if you remembered the light in the back room being on. I could swear neither of us..."

"Are you in the shop now?"

"Yeah. I stopped..."

"Get out. Right now." His voice sounded more like a growl. "And call Alex."

"But I'm not..."

"Now, Dakota."

I heard a box fall in the back room and I bolted out the front door. "I'll call you right back." I ended the call and immediately called Alex. He answered on the first ring which surprised me. I thought he would have let it go to voicemail. I blurted out that I thought someone was in the shop and, just as Declan had, he advised me to move out of harm's way and assured me he would be right over.

By the time we got off the phone, I was standing across the street, around the corner of the coffee shop. I had already missed two texts from Declan asking what was happening. I called him back to let him know I was okay.

"Hey. Alex is on his way over." From the angle I was at, I could see my shop but not the inside of it.

"Good. Where are you?"

"By the coffee shop, hiding but visible so I can see when he gets here. I'm sorry I hung up on you."

"No need to apologize. But what happened?"

I sighed into the phone. "I heard a box fall. I guess I'm still a little jumpy from this morning."

"Did you see anyone?"

"No. But now I feel kind of dumb for calling Alex. Maybe it really was just a box falling on its own."

"Can't be too careful. Besides, it wasn't just the box, it was the light, too. And it wasn't on this morning. I stopped and peeked in the windows on my way out of town."

Before I could respond, I saw Alex pull up and park two stores down. "Alex just got here."

"Okay. Call me back. Be safe."

Chapter 13

I stepped around the corner so Alex could see me. He brought one hand up to tell me to stay put and with the other, pushed a finger to his lips so I didn't shout out to him. I watched him peer into the window with his back pressed against the building and had to stifle a laugh. I understood the reasoning but thought it was something they only did in movies. He pulled open the front door and slipped inside.

He told me not to move but I kept inching closer, it felt like he had been inside for hours. Logically, I knew it was less than two minutes, but I'm impatient and had managed to cross the street and make it to the front door before he emerged.

He rolled his eyes and grunted. "I'm glad to see you know how to listen."

I shrugged. "You were in there a long time."

"So, you were going to rush in to protect me? What were you going to do, stab them in the face with a tattoo gun?"

"It's a tattoo machine and you clearly know nothing about them."

"You're right. What I do know is there was definitely someone here, but they left before I got here. You probably scared them away."

"Do you know how they got in?"

"They busted the lock on the back door."

I took out my phone and sent a message to Declan. He replied almost immediately with a picture of Diesel in the basket of a shopping cart, sitting next to a deadbolt lock. I had to give him credit for being a full step ahead.

"Who are you talking to?" Alex leaned forward in an attempt to see my screen and I pulled the phone away.

"Not that it's any of your business, but I was talking to Declan."

"Uh-huh. Where is your friend today?"

Before answering, I had to remind myself that he was here because I called him to help me. "He went to the city to pick up a security camera for my house." I braced myself for the question I knew was coming next.

"Why is he getting a camera for your house?"

I didn't realize until that moment how warm the day had gotten. "Because I had an unwanted visitor early this morning. It's possible it was just a random person passing by. I can't say for sure."

"Well, that explains why you didn't call me then. Did you have the shop cameras on so we can look to see who was here?"

I nodded yes and then to the door for him to follow me. "I never turn them off. I feel like it defeats the purpose of having them." I set my laptop on the counter, wondering why I hadn't thought to check it sooner.

The tension between the two of us was uncomfortable and I silently cursed at my laptop for being so slow to boot up. He was standing so close I could hear him breathing and I took two steps back. "So, any new news about Maggie?"

"I wouldn't tell you even if I had some." He didn't bother to look in my direction. "What were you doing here today?"

"Are you kidding? I was in the area, so I stopped by. I don't think I need a reason to be at my own place of employment, especially when I own it."

"Right. How did your sleuthing go?" He put his hand up to keep me from responding right away. "There's no need to deny it. I saw you going into the realtor office and since you already own a house and business..."

"Ooh, look at you playing detective." He spun around and stared at me while I smirked at him. "Did you ever think maybe Declan is looking to move here?"

He let out a hearty laugh and it was the first time I noticed he had a sense of humor. "That thought did cross my mind, but I don't think he'd be looking to buy."

"What does that mean?"

He turned back to look at my laptop. "Can you pull up the camera feed?"

I didn't move. "Yes. As soon as you tell me what you mean by that."

He huffed and crossed his arms. "If you haven't noticed the way he looks at you, maybe you're not as good of a detective as you think you are. Now, can you pull up the feed?"

I ignored what he said but only verbally. For twenty minutes we stared at the laptop screen, playing the same clip over and over, hoping we may have just missed the one second when the suspect showed their face.

"This is proving to be useless. Whoever they are, they're smart." He leaned against the counter, arms crossed again, and stared at me. "You want to tell me what happened this morning?"

"Not really. There's also not much to tell. It was early, still dark. Diesel was growling..."

"Diesel?"

"Declan's cat. Anyway, I heard a noise, like a twig snapping, Diesel ran off and I saw someone running across the street toward the lake. It was only the outline of a person that I could see."

"Do you know for sure that Declan is in the city right now?"

An angry laugh escaped my lips. "You're kidding, right?"

His only response was to raise his eyebrows.

"Yes, I know he's in the city. You can check his receipts when he gets back. Besides, Declan was passed out on my couch when I saw the person in my back yard and Diesel never would have growled at him." Alex still didn't respond and I was curious how he went from 'Declan likes you' to 'he may be guilty.' "I'm not sure why you're asking about him. Someone murdered Maggie before he got to town. He wasn't here when someone tagged the outside of my shop. He only offered to stay after he realized how many people believe I can be guilty, after someone threw a rock with a threatening message through my window. He's here to keep me safe."

"Keep you safe? Or keep you close?"

Every muscle in my body tightened. "Thank you for coming to check on the shop. You can go now." I closed the laptop and walked to the door to hold it open for him.

Alex hesitated but took the hint. He paused beside me on his way out. "I want to see those receipts when Declan gets back."

I didn't feel comfortable at the shop by myself and that idea made me angry. I spent my entire life seeking comfort in my art. My shop was like a second home to me and I was not okay with not being able to relax here.

I went to the back room and picked up the box that had fallen, thankful it was only paper towels for the bathroom and not something that needed to remain sterile. There was something to be said for being an organized person. I housed all my supplies, apart from paper products, in a large, metal storage cabinet with various sized drawers. Small slots on the front allowed for easy labeling. I also kept a metal desk for filing paperwork. I could have replaced it with a large filing cabinet but sometimes I preferred to stay in the back and work at the desk rather than being at the front counter where people could see me as they walked by.

The desk was much heavier when it was full. I emptied all the files before moving it from one shop to the other. Even with it full, I managed to push it across the concrete floor and against the back door. It wasn't the best security system, especially since I could move it myself, but I felt better knowing I tried. I made sure the drawers were locked and then locked the door between the shop and back room.

I tucked my laptop under my arm and left through the front door, laughing to myself as I slid the key in the lock to secure it. It seemed pointless. I left my Jeep where I parked it and walked past the gift shop and the diner to the bakery. I knew they had tables set up for patrons, but I had never seen anyone sitting inside. I hadn't been to the bakery yet, but I thought it might be the perfect spot to collect my thoughts and relax for a few minutes.

The mix of icing and fresh bread slapped me in the face when I opened the door and my stomach grumbled. I didn't see anyone at the front counter, but I heard a voice call out from the back telling me they would be right out. I took a glance at the menu on the wall and turned my attention to the display case. Every item seemed to be calling my name. How was anyone supposed to choose between the muffins, danish, and cannoli?

"Good morning. How can I help you?"

The voice was much deeper than the one I heard a moment ago and I flinched at the sound. "You scared me. Yours isn't the voice I heard when I came in."

"Oh, sorry. That was my boss. Do you need to speak to her?"

"No. I was just surprised, dreaming about pastries, I guess." I ordered a coffee and an orange-cranberry scone and made myself comfortable at one of the small, white tables. They looked more like something you would see on a rundown patio and didn't send a very welcoming message. Instead, they screamed 'you can stay if you want, but we'd prefer you didn't.'

I sent a quick text to Declan to let him know where I was and then opened my laptop to look up the addresses for Laura and Leyland. I could have done it the easy way and asked Celeste while I was at the realtor's office, but I thought I might be pressing my luck.

I typed their addresses into my phone and finally jotted down what I had found out about them. I had so many places I needed to go; I wasn't sure where to start. I needed to visit both Laura and Leyland, I had to go back to Andrew's, I really wanted to talk to Carly again, and I needed to see if I could convince Caleb to talk to me without Carly being around. I hoped to be able to find them all.

I put all my papers back in their folder and stood to leave when Roxanne came out of the back.

"Oh, good, you're still here." She looked down and saw all my belongings in my hands. "Do you have a minute to talk? I've been meaning to stop by your shop, but I know you were busy. I'm also not sure what the proper etiquette is for a place like that." A light pink splashed her cheeks, embarrassment due to lack of knowledge.

"Oh, you don't need to worry about that. People stop by all the time just to say 'hi.' Some people come in to check out the atmosphere and cleanliness before requesting an appointment. You don't really need a reason to come in."

"Now I wish I didn't put that much thought into it. Anyway, I don't want to take a lot of your time, but I heard you were asking people questions about Maggie."

"I am. It's not something I'm enjoying, but I'd never be able to relax if I didn't at least try."

"I don't think I would be able to relax even with trying. You're a stronger person than I am."

I watched her shoulders sag when she said that, but I had no idea how to respond. I always wanted to be supportive, but the right words never came to me and it was hard when I didn't understand what they were going through. "What did you want to talk to me about?"

"I figure your focus is probably on the usual suspects like Annette because she's terrible. Also, the boyfriend, the best friend, the ex-boyfriend. But I think you should look a little further than her immediate circle."

"What makes you say that?" I didn't find it necessary to tell her we were already expanding outward.

"I'm not really comfortable telling you why and if anyone asks, you didn't hear it from me."

She waited until I agreed to tell me anything more. "You should talk to Nikki Goodwin. I'll go as far as to say her and Maggie weren't on the best of terms."

"Interesting. We haven't spoken to her yet, but we did meet Kerry yesterday and she told us to talk to Nikki, too. Although, I'm going to guess it's not for the same reason."

"Probably not."

The bakery was in desperate need of repair. The paint showed chips and scuff marks from the tables and chairs rubbing against the wall. The counters and floors were clean and it was clear Roxanne cared about the cleanliness, she just didn't put as much attention on the upkeep. The building itself was solid. I knew because I could barely hear the bikes as they pulled into the slanted parking slots outside the bakery. Normally, I could recognize that sound from a block away.

I thanked Roxanne for her help and excused myself. Outside, I found Clyde, Falcon, Nick, and Wyatt waiting for me. "What are you all doing here?" I hugged each of them. "I didn't think I would see any of you again for months."

"Declan called in reinforcements." After all the years of being friends, I still had no idea where Falcon got his name from.

"For what?"

Falcon shrugged. "He didn't say. He just said he wanted a protective detail so we're here."

"Regardless of the reason, I'm glad you're all here. I felt awful about not being able to spend any time with you last weekend."

"You know better than to feel bad about that. So, where are you heading next? I'll follow you."

Chapter 14

Falcon followed me to Leyland's house while the rest of the guys went to check into the hotel. It was a modest ranch, much smaller than I would have thought considering the size of their childhood home. The house transferred to Laura was a mansion, the only one in town. It also sat on the largest amount of land anyone in town owned. Leyland's looked to be the same size as mine but with new windows and a fresh coat of paint. I wondered about the drastic difference between the homes and why Laura got the family home and Leyland didn't.

The sound of a running lawnmower came from behind the house and the smell of cut grass lingered in the air. A white fence bordered the property; I let myself in through the gate and walked to the back of the house. I stood at the corner, waiting for Leyland to finish the lap he was on and waved when he looked over.

He nodded, stopped the push mower, and walked toward me, wiping sweat off his face with his t-shirt. "Dakota? Do you make a habit of wandering through people's fences?"

"No, uh, I..."

A smile spread across his face. "I'm kidding. There's no way I would have heard you if you went to the door."

"Oh. Yeah, I didn't think you would. You know you really shouldn't be mowing the lawn with a new tattoo. It's stirring up all kinds of dirt that can get inside the wound."

"I covered it, loosely. I don't imagine you make follow-up house calls to all your clients. What do I owe the pleasure?"

His body language and facial expression told me he was okay with my presence but didn't trust my motive. He had good instincts. "I wanted to ask you about your relationship with your sister and about your childhood home. Specifically, why she's living in it and you're not."

"Oh." He wiped sweat from his face again, this time from nervousness and not exhaustion. "I didn't really want the house. It's okay that she has it." His eyes darted side to side but he never looked at me.

"But she got the house for free. I understand you had to purchase your own. That doesn't bother you?"

He stuffed his hands in the pockets of his shorts. "No." His eyes shifted toward me and he stared into mine. "For the past three years, my sister has been groveling with my parents for forgiveness. She got the house, but she gets nothing else. I get the rest of the inheritance. Their money, cars, vacation home, it'll all come to me."

I nodded along with his words. "Laura threatened them? Tried to blackmail them?"

"Nope. Lost everything because she fell in love."

I didn't expect that. "I don't suppose you'd like to elaborate?"

"She was engaged to a man she met on the internet. She fell in love before she even met him in person. My parents hated him and thought he was just in it for the money. So, they threatened to cut her out of the will if she married him."

"What did she do?"

"She told them if they gave her the house, she wouldn't ever ask them for another dime. Saying my parents were livid is an understatement. But Laura signed all the paperwork and my parents walked away. The only problem was her fiancé was only in it for the money. Once he found out what she did, he left. My sister gave up everything for a man she barely knew and it all blew up in her face."

"Has she had any luck getting your parents back on her side?" I caught movement in the distance and doing my best not to draw attention, glanced at the far side of the house. Falcon crouched at the corner, twisting his head so he could see both of us without Leyland being able to see him.

"Not at all. My sister is naive enough to believe my parents will give in with time, feel bad for her because the guy left."

"You don't think they will?"

"I know they won't. They are not forgiving people. They feel betrayed and nothing Laura does will be able to fix that."

"Do you know who Veronica Tandy is?"

"No. Uh, you said that name when I went to the shop. She had an appointment at the same time as Maggie."

I couldn't tell by his tone if he knew who she was or not. When he was at the shop, he didn't give any indication that he recognized the name. "Maggie is Veronica. Veronica Tandy is a pseudonym that she used to write a blog that made a lot of people mad."

His eyes narrowed and he bit his bottom lip. "I don't understand. Maggie is a nice person...was." His body withered when he corrected himself. It was a natural reaction but not one I would expect if he had murdered her.

"Detective Landry took her laptop. He verified that Maggie did write the posts. I've read a lot of them and I think there may have been a side to her that you didn't know."

"I don't want to hear about this. I loved Maggie for the person I knew her to be. I don't ever want anything to change that. I think you should leave."

I sighed. "If you change your mind, you know how to find me." I left him standing all alone in the middle of his yard and I wondered if I had just ruined the image he had of his high school love.

Falcon met me by my Jeep.

"How'd it go?"

"You tell me. You watched the whole thing."

"I can't protect you if I can't see you."

"I appreciate you being here, but I really don't need protection. Declan is just worried because he's not here, but there's really no reason for him to worry."

"He told us someone threatened you. That's the best reason I can think of for him to be worried."

I have never been one to think I needed protection from anything and I didn't like this much attention. In theory, it was nice, but feeling like I had a bodyguard made me more uncomfortable than knowing someone may want to harm me. "He's overprotective."

"Well, we can't leave now. You know no one says 'no' to Declan."

He wasn't wrong. "At least I'm stuck with you guys. It could be worse."

My next stop was Laura's house. I wanted to see if her story checked out with what Leyland had told me. The house sat at the edge of town behind a sprawling iron fence. The front gate was open, so I took that as an open invitation and drove in. Flowering trees lined the driveway which fell in a circle at the front of the house. It would have been a long walk for Falcon, so he followed me right up to the house.

I barely had my door open when I heard Laura yelling from the entryway. She circled the back of my Jeep and met me as soon as I stepped out. Her cheeks burned pink and her hands balled into fists. Her voice was a choked screech, much as one would expect from someone experiencing a bout of hysteria. "I thought I told you to stay away from my brother? Do you have any idea how much you upset him?"

"I only stopped by to ask him about his house."

"But you told him about Maggie and her blog. He didn't need to know about that."

Leyland must have called her as soon as we left. "I assumed he already knew. I didn't tell him with any malicious intent."

"Yeah, well, he didn't know but he does now, thanks to you."

"How did you find out? Did she tell you?"

That question quieted her and she stood, dumbfounded. "Uh, no. Not exactly." With her answer, she changed from that strong, confident person I saw in the diner a few nights ago to a small, unsure child.

A part of me felt bad for her when I saw the change. "How did you find out?"

She thrust her hands in her pockets and stared at the ground. "I was one of her followers. I always loved how she was so willing to call people out when they did something wrong; until one of her posts hit a little too close to me."

"That was the one about your house, right?"

She nodded. "We like to keep our private life private. When my parents left, we told everyone they were moving to their vacation home. No one knew about my fiancé or the agreement we made." She glanced at me with tears in her eyes. "Leyland told me everything he told you. Anyway, she posted about an anonymous person, saying she would tell the entire town for no other reason than to embarrass the person. I responded and told her I didn't think it was fair to do that to someone and she told me she did think it was fair because I was only thinking of myself and not taking my brother into consideration."

"Oh. So, she knew it was you who responded?"

"She did. When she realized what she had done, she deleted her response. I didn't know it was her blog until that comment. She was the only person I could think of that would have come to my brother's defense so fast. So, I went and confronted her about it."

While I waited for her to continue, I watched Falcon pace back and forth across the manicured lawn. He kept his head down, typing into his phone, only glancing over every few seconds.

"The confrontation didn't go well at the beginning, but we did come to an agreement; if I didn't tell people her real identity, she wouldn't post my story. It worked in favor of both of us."

"She never told anyone?"

"She didn't say a word. And now, I guess I don't have to worry about it anymore."

"Do you know how she found out to begin with?"

She huffed and rolled her eyes. "I'm guessing my dear brother. She was everything to him."

I thanked her for speaking to me and apologized for the intrusion before waving Falcon over to take our leave.

When we got back to the road, I pulled over to decide what to do next.

"Declan is at your house. He's setting up the camera for you. He also got a motion activated light for your front and back doors."

"Hopefully, that will deter someone if they get too close to the house. I guess we should go meet him there. I'd like to get something to eat, too. I'm starving."

"He brought lunch back with him."

"Ooh. Then we're definitely going back to my house. Speaking of food, Fiona called me on our way to Laura's and asked if I wanted to go to her house for a small cookout tonight. I told her I had guests and she said we are all welcome."

Falcon raised his eyebrows. "Fiona? That's the redhead from the coffee shop, right?"

I nodded.

"No need to ask me twice."

Chapter 15

Declan and Nick had just finished mounting the camera when we arrived at my house. They already had the motion activated lights Declan purchased put up near both the front and back doors. Wyatt lounged in a chair, looking at the lake across the street.

"I didn't expect you to put everything up for me, I would have done it."

"I don't mind. I like doing little projects like this. Although, I'd prefer to do something like this as a precaution rather than a necessity."

"Well, I appreciate it. Thank you."

"I'll need your laptop to finish everything up. But I can do it..." A vicious knock at the front door interrupted the rest of his sentence. "How much do you want to bet that's your detective at the door."

I rolled my eyes. "I think he's here more than I am."

Nick ushered Alex through the house. "Dakota, someone is here to see you."

"Yeah, thanks." I forced a smile. "How can we help you this time?"

Alex looked around the deck. "You have a houseful, huh? Did you hire a moving company?"

My eyes narrowed. "I hired a few people to help me move the heavy stuff into and out of the truck. I moved the rest myself. Why?"

"Did you provide the supplies? The straps and blankets?"

I had no idea why that would matter. "I did. They're in my hall closet."

He leaned against the railing and crossed his arms. "I'm going to need those. I finally got the autopsy results back. The killer strangled Maggie with a strap, typically used for moving."

I raised my eyebrows. "Well, my instincts were correct about her not drowning. I do have to say, I'm surprised you didn't bust through the door with a search warrant."

He reached behind him and pulled a folded piece of paper from his pocket. "I have one. I was just hoping I didn't have to use it."

"You don't. I'll go get them." I walked down the hall and opened the closet door. I stored all the moving blankets and straps on the top shelf, assuming I wouldn't need them again any time soon. I couldn't reach the straps, so I grabbed the bottom blanket and pulled, causing the entire pile to crash to the floor. I left the blankets in a heap on the floor and handed the strap storage bag to Alex. "Here you go."

He nodded at me. "Thank you for your cooperation."

"I have nothing to hide."

"Yeah. The lab will tell me if that's true or not." He turned and walked out the door, not acknowledging that there were any other people there.

Wyatt flashed me a sad smile. "I'm willing to bet ninety-five percent of people in this town own ratchet straps. It's just coincidence that you happen to be the last one that moved here. He'll figure it out soon enough."

All the guys were staring at me. "It's not that easy. I argued with her the night before she died. Detective Landry found her necklace in my shop. I'm the last one who moved here and someone strangled her with moving straps. And she had a piece of my flash art, that I hadn't distributed, in her possession when they found her. I need to find the real killer fast."

Declan and I spent the next hour verbalizing what we knew so far while the other guys tried to piece everything together. We thought it might help to have someone with fresh eyes and fresh ears, but they all came to the same suspects that we already had.

We all pulled in front of Fiona's house ten minutes late. I rode with Declan and the rest of the guys followed us. Alex's visit flustered all of us and none of us were really in the mood to be social with anyone outside our immediate circle. I liked Fiona and already felt like we had become friends. I didn't want to let her down by not coming over. Plus, there were already a lot of people here. I could use this barbecue to my advantage and talk to several people during a short span of time.

Fiona stuck her head out her front door and waved. "Dakota, you made it. Come on in." She ushered us all in through the bright red front door. It matched the front shutters that paired perfectly with the cream siding. "You can all head out back. There are a lot more people than I expected considering it was such short notice. There is food and drinks. We have a few people working the grill; just let them know what you want."

Once they walked outside, Fiona turned to me. "I hope you don't mind, I invited everyone. I'm not trying to intrude or make you uncomfortable, but I thought it could help you if everyone was all in the same place. There isn't a person in this town that will pass up the opportunity to come to a social event, even if it is in someone's back yard."

"It's actually perfect. And, if this was your plan, I will never be able to express how much I appreciate it."

"You can thank me after you figure this mess out. Let's get some food."

My jaw dropped when I stepped onto her patio. The back yard was stunning. From the front of the house, one would never expect something so grandiose. From the street, the house had a comfortable, cottage feel to it. I expected some rose bushes and an ivy-covered arbor. What I found was an entertainment area that I imagined was better suited for a multi-million-dollar mansion. I walked out to a cement patio with cabanas set up in both corners of the house. An in-ground pool ran half the length of the yard and ended with a hot tub. A grill and tables covered in bowls of food lined the fence. Groups of people dotted the yard; some occupying the wicker furniture of love seats, chairs, and ottomans. Others were enjoying the pool and the rest were standing in small groups chatting and eating off overflowing paper plates.

I recognized quite a few people and there were some I had never met or seen. I wasn't much of a social person, especially in crowds, so I was thankful to see the guys I came with all standing in a group together. I asked for a burger and filled my plate with a variety of salads before moving out of the way so I could scan the yard. She wasn't there when I looked the first time, but Mitzi had found Declan and stood with her arm linked with his, her other hand grasping his forearm. As usual, Diesel stood perched on his shoulder.

While I ate, I looked over the crowd to see who I recognized and who I had an interest in speaking with. Annette and Carly were engaged in conversation. Laura and Leyland chatted with Caleb. I considered joining their conversation once I finished eating. I'd love to hear what Maggie's ex and current, or most recent, boyfriend had to talk about. I wished there were a way to get closer to them so I could eavesdrop, but it seemed to be the only group not packed beside others.

I dumped my empty plate and plastic fork in the trash can standing against the back of the house and made my way over to Fiona.

"Hey. I was going to come find you in a minute. Have you met Roxanne?"

I nodded. "Just this morning. It's nice to see you again." We all chatted for a few minutes, mostly about Maggie. They were discussing possible motives for her death, but I didn't add to the conversation. They didn't offer any information that I didn't already know. "Fiona, I was hoping you might be able to introduce me to a few people. There are a lot of people here I haven't met yet."

"Of course. Roxanne, we'll catch up later?"

"Sure. I'll see you two later." She walked away to join a different conversation.

"I'm not sure who you've met and who you haven't. Is there anyone in particular that you want me to introduce you to?"

I glanced over her shoulder and locked eyes with Declan. He mouthed the word 'help' and I laughed. Mitzi still had his right arm in her grasp and Celeste stood on his left. I replayed our conversation from earlier and wondered if she really was willing to fight Mitzi for Declan's attention. I laughed again at the thought. "I think we should go save Declan before we do anything else."

She looked over to see what I was talking about. "Oh, that poor guy. Of course, not that you have to worry about Mitzi, but don't be surprised if she shows up at your door with muffins and cookies and doesn't allow you to have any."

"Thank you for the warning. But you do know Declan and I are friends, right?"

"Oh...honey." She shook her head but didn't finish the sentence. "Let's go save your *friend*."

I didn't ask her to elaborate but everyone in this town seemed to believe it was impossible for a male and female to be in a platonic relationship. I had been friends with this group for over ten years and I'd never dated any of them.

While we walked over, I noticed the solar powered lights had turned on. Tall ones stood along the fence and shorter ones lined the area around the pool. I had to give her credit for the layout. It was the perfect spot for entertaining. I also noticed Nikki and Kerry were standing with Declan and I assumed Kerry had brought her wife over specifically to introduce them.

"You finally came to join us." Declan used my appearance to unhook his arm from Mitzi's grasp and he stood next to me, wrapping his arm around my waist. "You remember Kerry? This is Nikki. I've already told her we were going to try to catch up with her."

"Hi. It's nice to meet you."

"You, too. Kerry said you might come talk to me. Was there something specific you were looking for?"

Nikki was not what I expected after meeting Kerry. I made assumptions that I shouldn't have. I didn't take kindly to people assuming things about me or my friends. I don't know exactly what I expected but it wasn't her. She was tall with deep brown hair and tanned skin. She wore skinny jeans with a suede ankle boot and a buttoned blouse.

"I was interested in what you might be able to tell me about Maggie. I heard, straight from the source, that she was Annette's niece and someone told me to talk to you about it. I also heard from someone else that the two of you weren't on the best terms."

"Both sources are correct. I do need to apologize to you first, Kerry, because I didn't tell you exactly what I knew. I was friends with Maggie. We didn't get together often but we would go to the city occasionally. Being on the swim team came with strict rules and no alcohol topped the list. So, we would go out for a couple glasses of wine and some sushi. The city was far enough away that she didn't think we would run into anyone that would tell Andrew."

"Were you close friends?"

"Close? I liked her, she was fun to go out with and talk to. But she thought we were much closer than we actually were. She confided in me about writing her blog and told me the reactions it got amused her. The reality was, she was hurting a lot of people, potentially, at least."

Everyone in our group stared at her in anticipation. "What did you do when she told you?"

"I told her she needed to stop but she argued that people should know the truth. I began to look at her differently at that point. I didn't feel I could trust her anymore and when the truth came out, I didn't want my name associated with her in any way. Call me selfish."

"How did you find out about her and Annette? It seems like everyone in this town knows everything about everyone, yet Maggie was able to keep her secret about her blog and her relatives."

"She was very good at keeping her life private. Somehow, she wormed her way into other people's lives and learned way more about them than she should know. She told me, in confidence, that Annette was her aunt, but she also has another relative in town and I have no idea who it could be."

Mitzi had been quiet until that point. "Well, if you ask me, with those hair-brained articles and attitude of her and her aunt, I would be looking for someone who is as cold and heartless as they are."

"The only other person I can think of that meets those requirements is Caleb and I certainly hope him and Maggie weren't related." Fiona scrunched her face. "Dakota's right, though. In a town where you can't sneeze without everyone knowing, it's odd that there are people who are related and we don't know about it."

"Sounds to me like that's where we need to look. We need to find the other relation then figure out why they are hiding it." I looked across our group and saw it had grown since Fiona and I joined. "Falcon, I didn't see you come over. Uh, have you met everyone? This is Celeste, Mitzi, Kerry, Nikki, Leyland, and Fiona. This is Falcon." Even in the dark with only the solar light from the perimeter, I saw Falcon and Fiona lock eyes.

Falcon was always a little different when it came to women and it was rare to see him take interest in one. I had a strong feeling he might be sticking around longer than he planned.

Diesel hung over Declan's shoulder, sleeping. He woke and did the best he could to stretch his back and paws in such a small space. He laid his ears flat against his head and the low growl I heard first thing this morning returned. Declan reached up to scratch the cat's head and he calmed at the touch. I looked around us, making a mental note of everyone who was around, wondering why he was growling again. I felt Nick and Clyde walk up and close in behind me. Apparently, everyone trusted Diesel's instincts. After Declan managed to lull him into a state of contented purring, the conversation picked up again.

Kerry looked at Declan with her eyes wide. "It doesn't bother you that he's growling like that when he's that close to your face?"

Before he could answer, Mitzi stepped forward. "My dear. I'm sure he's quite used to it. Have you seen the cat? Pitiful thing must be angry all the time about looking like that. Have you seen his ears? It could pick up satellite radio with those things."

Diesel yowled.

"Oh, relax you wrinkled, old bag. At least you have pretty eyes."

"Fiona, may I use your bathroom?" As soon as I asked, Diesel hopped from Declan's shoulder to mine.

"Of course. First door on the left in the hallway."

I noticed the hall when we walked through the house earlier, it was off the dining room, opposite of where it was in mine. From my first step toward the house, Clyde was on my heels. I stopped walking and he ran straight into the back of me, causing Diesel to dig his claws into my shoulder. "As much as I appreciate the escort, maybe you can give me a few inches of space? Walk beside me or something." The comment came out harsher than I meant it, but he knew I had issues when it came to personal space. I never liked people touching me or standing too close and there were only a select few that I welcomed any sort of touch from. It was one of the biggest issues I faced with my job because I had to touch people all the time.

His tone hinted at amusement. "Sorry. Just following orders." He moved to my side.

"What exactly did Declan tell you all to make you act this way?"

"Exactly what we told you earlier. He didn't give specifics; just said you weren't to be alone."

"Even to go to the bathroom?"

"He was adamant."

I turned the corner to go down the hall and Diesel yowled, jumped to the floor, and ran toward what I assumed was a bedroom. "Diesel. Get back here." It was dark in the hallway but the light from the dining room was bright enough for me to see which room he ran into. "Diesel?" The dining room didn't afford the same light to the room as it did the hall, so I pulled my phone from my pocket, turned on the flashlight, and gasped. Diesel was sitting on the floor at the foot of the bed, right next to a pair of legs sticking out from behind it.

Chapter 16

Clyde ushered me back to the hallway with instructions to call an ambulance while he went back to check for a pulse. I was giving the dispatcher the address when I heard Clyde shout that she was still alive but unconscious. Declan and Fiona entered the hall and Fiona wrapped her arm around my shoulder while Declan entered the bedroom.

I had just ended the call when Alex appeared in front of me. "Where is she?"

I pointed to the bedroom.

He pointed back at me. "You don't move. Fiona, you go stand outside and don't let anyone leave the property. Everyone is a suspect until we prove otherwise, or she wakes up and tells us."

Alex banished the three of us to the dining room when the paramedics came in. Once they took the victim outside, Alex came out and sat with us, notebook and pen in hand.

"Dakota, it's so strange meeting you in this sort of circumstance again. Which one of you found the victim?"

I sighed and my feet twitched beneath the table. "I did. Well, technically, Diesel did. Clyde was with me."

"That's convenient. Who's Clyde."

"That's me."

Alex let his pen fall and rolled his eyes in Clyde's direction. "Right. Glad you seem so happy to be here. What are you doing in town, Clyde?"

"Protective detail for Dakota."

I felt Declan tense beside me.

"Protective detail? For Dakota? What exactly are you protecting her from?"

"Whoever it is that's messin' with her. No one is going to hurt her as long as we're around."

"Mhm." He retrieved his pen and wrote in his notebook. "Is that why you tried to strangle Carly tonight?"

"Not really my style, detective."

"What exactly is your style, Clyde?" Every time he said his name, he drew it out like he was trying to intimidate him by using it.

"I've always been more of a knife guy. Switchblades, satu, bowies…"

I buried my face in my hands and whispered to myself. "Oh, please, please stop talking."

"Dakota? Are you still with us? Why don't you tell me what happened."

"I came inside to use the bathroom. I had Diesel with me. Clyde followed me in."

"Why did he do that?"

"One of the guys has been with me all day. Well, since they got to town anyway."

"So, you came inside with the psychic cat and a security guard. Go on."

"Diesel jumped off my shoulder and ran down the hall. I called to him and followed him to the bedroom. I saw a person lying there and called for an ambulance." I knew how this must look to him. I was already a suspect in one murder and I had just discovered a second person someone tried to kill. No matter what I said, things did not look good for me.

"Where were the three of you before you came inside?"

"We were all outside chatting with a group of people."

"How did Declan and Fiona end up inside?"

I was going to let Declan answer that question, but Clyde jumped on it instead.

"I texted Declan and told him to come in with Fiona. I asked for her because it's her house and for him because he would have killed me if I didn't have him come in."

"Annnd there it is. You know I adore you, Clyde, but please stop talking." I watched him try to suppress a smile.

"Are you afraid he'll say something he shouldn't?"

"No. I know he always says things he has no business saying simply because he likes to stir the pot."

A uniformed officer came through the back door. "Detective Landry? I got the list of attendees from the owner, at least everyone she can remember. The only three people who are no longer here are a Carly Evans, an Annette Nicholson, and a Leyland Bailey."

"The paramedics just transported Carly to the hospital. Annette won't go far; she works for the mayor at the town hall. Have someone go find Leyland and bring him to the station."

Alex dismissed us but allowed us to talk to Fiona and Falcon before we left, supervised, of course. When we got out to the bikes, Declan asked Clyde to bring me home. He wanted to take the long way around to check on the shop before going back to my house. I knew better. He wanted to blow off some steam.

"Be careful, okay?"

"You know I will." He handed me a helmet and gave Diesel's to Clyde before kissing my forehead. "I'll be there soon."

Declan arrived at the house twenty minutes after we got there. It was a small town and much more time than he needed, even for the long way, but I only cared that he made it back safely. I always needed time alone after being with too many people for too long. Declan was the opposite. Out of the entire crew, he was the most sociable. He loved having family and friends around him and would fall into a mild state of depression if he spent too much time by himself. He knew he needed time by himself when he started to get angry. Rather than express that emotion in front of others, he withdrew and took the time he needed to cool down.

I respected his knowledge of his needs and never asked questions or for an explanation. When he came in, I gave him a hug just to let him know how glad I was that he was there. He didn't say anything, but I knew he appreciated it.

"I caught up with Nick and Wyatt when they got back to the hotel. Falcon and Fiona are still at her place. She's going to stay at the hotel with him tonight since her house is a crime scene. Oh, and Carly is awake. She's going to be fine."

"Does she know who tried to kill her?"

"He can't say for sure because he was eavesdropping and only catching part of the conversation, but Wyatt doesn't think so."

"Great. After Alex's visit earlier today, that doesn't make me feel any better." I flung myself into the over-sized chair that was large enough for me to curl up and nap in. "What am I supposed to do?"

"You keep doing what you always do. You're in a tough situation but that doesn't change how strong you are."

"It's not that easy. Every piece of evidence Alex has points to me. I know someone is trying to set me up, but Alex doesn't, and they're doing an excellent job of it. I don't know how to fix it."

"It is that easy because you have a full support group behind you. And I've seen you do it before. Alex may not have what he needs yet, but he will eventually have to admit that he's wrong about you." Declan stared at me until I nodded in agreement. "What are we doing tomorrow?"

"I want to go see Annette again before we do anything else. I have an appointment at six and barely have half an outline to show my client, so I need to get the drawing done. And I had a list of people I was hoping to talk to tonight but, obviously, plans changed for that, so I'd like to do that tomorrow, as well."

"All right. We'll go get some sleep now, visit Annette in the morning, and then you can work on your drawing for a while and Clyde and I will try to figure out who Maggie's other relative is. One of her blogs may contain the answer, but we didn't notice because we weren't looking for it."

"Sleep sounds like a great idea. I'm exhausted." I grabbed Harley from the back of the couch and took her to the bedroom with me, surprised she was showing her face. I think she liked Clyde.

Clyde stayed on the couch and Declan slept in my room. I fell asleep almost instantly and don't remember him coming in. I knew Declan could sleep through a bomb going off during the first few hours, but the longer he slept, the easier it was to wake him. I did my best to slide off the bed and slip out of the room as quietly as I could.

I found Clyde in the kitchen, leaning against the sink with a coffee mug in hand. "Trouble sleeping?" I filled my own mug from the pot he made.

"Not at all. I'm ex-military, remember? A thirty-minute power nap can get me through the next two days."

"Must be nice." I nodded my head toward the door for him to follow me.

"It comes in handy. But you can't do it often. You'll start hallucinating from the lack of sleep. That's a bad thing, especially when your life may be in danger."

"I can only imagine. What's you do the rest of the night?"

"Watched a little TV, ate a sandwich, read some of Maggie's blog posts. You know, she was pretty funny."

"She was mean and ruthless."

"I didn't say she wasn't. But she was also kind of funny."

We both sat, staring into the darkness. It seemed like so long ago that I saw a figure in the shadows. It didn't feel like it was only yesterday; so much had happened since then and it was strange to think that, for those few minutes, I was afraid to be in my own backyard. "Hey. Why didn't the lights come on when we came out here?"

"Because Declan is smart. He angled the sensors higher so they would capture movement closer to the perimeter of the deck. The cameras have a wider angle, so they'll pick up movement from the bottom of the stairs all the way to the door."

"Good thinking on his part."

"You know how he is; always three steps ahead of everyone else and does things right the first time."

Clyde could be a loose cannon at times, always the first to get in someone's face or talk way too much in front of police officers. I never figured out whether it was from adrenaline, nerves, or a little of both. The one thing I did know for sure was that his loyalty never faltered. If a person were lucky enough to get him on their side, he would remain there forever.

"I know I was giving you a hard time yesterday but I'm glad you're here. And I appreciate you coming out when Declan called."

"You know we've got your back."

My eyes finally adjusted to the dark and I looked over at him, surprised not only to see a cat curled up in his lap, but to realize it wasn't Diesel. "What did you do to my cat? Harley doesn't even sit with me, never mind curl up on my lap."

He stroked her fur and she rolled over so he could rub her belly, purring loud enough for me to hear. "Have you ever heard the saying about animals being able to sense evil?"

"Yeah."

"Well, maybe it's true."

"Do you remember a minute ago when I told you I'm glad you're here?"

"Yeah."

"Well, I lied."

Chapter 17

I didn't ask Clyde what his plans were for the day, but he left the house about thirty minutes before Declan and I did. After the events of last night, Declan refused to even let me go inside the town hall by myself. Even though it was a public place, he didn't believe there would be enough people and he reminded me that the entire town was at Fiona's last night and someone still attacked Carly. I couldn't argue with him.

We walked into the office and found a petite, blonde woman behind the counter.

"Good morning. How may I assist you?" She had a southern drawl and a voice so high pitched it made my shoulders tense when she spoke.

"Hi. We were hoping to speak with Annette."

She took a quick breath in and her shoulders sagged as she let it out. "Oh, well, I'm afraid that's not possible today. Annette has taken a vacation. That's why I'm here." She dressed like she had just stepped off the set of a 1980's music video. Multiple bangle bracelets clanked on both her wrists; gold hoops hung from her ears. She had her hair pulled into a high ponytail and a patterned sweatband wrapped around her head. "She went to visit family."

I swatted Declan's leg with the back of my hand to make sure he was paying attention. "Do you know when she'll be back?"

Before she could answer, Alex walked through the door with Mitzi at his heels. "Dakota, what are you doing here?"

"I could ask you the same thing. I thought you preferred to make house calls."

"That's not an answer."

"We came to talk to Annette." I leaned to the side so I could see around him. "Good morning, Mitzi."

Her face grew into a smile large enough to almost hide the rest of her features. "Good morning to you, Miss Dakota. And it certainly is a good morning for me. Hello, Declan. I must say you do look even better without your bald spot."

Declan tried to suppress a laugh and all that came out was a grunt. "Mitzi."

"Ha. See that? I'm already starting to wear you down."

"Enough. Mitzi, you need to go home and take a cold shower. Dakota, Diesel...uh, Declan, you both need to go about your business somewhere other than here." He turned toward the woman behind the counter. "Do I know you? It doesn't matter. I need to see Annette Nicholson, please." He pulled his badge from his pocket and showed it to her. "Detective Alex Landry."

I put effort into not bursting out laughing. All I did was talk to Mitzi and he completely lost control of the room. He grew flustered and it showed.

"As I was just explaining to this lovely couple, Annette had gone on vacation. I'm filling in."

"Uh, huh. Do you know where she went? I stopped at her house first and she wasn't there."

"I'm afraid I can't say. I'm just filling in."

"Do you have any idea when she'll be back?"

"I can't answer that for sure, either."

I could see the muscles in his jaw clenching and he squeezed his eyes shut.

"Okay. If you hear from her, tell her to call me." He pulled a business card out of his wallet and tossed it on the front counter before turning to leave.

I practically pushed Mitzi out of my way to catch up with Alex. "Detective?"

He didn't slow his step at all. "I told you to stay out of this, Dakota."

"I'm allowed to talk to people."

"Not when I know you're here specifically to ask questions about the case, you're not."

"Do you have any idea who that woman was?"

He continued down the hall without looking at me. "No."

"You don't think that's weird that none of us know who she is? Everyone knows everyone here. I've been here a week and know almost everyone."

He finally stopped and looked at me. "What is your point?"

"My point is...there is a strange woman working in the town hall and no one knows where Annette is. Before you got there, she told us Annette took a vacation to visit family."

"So?"

"So? She didn't tell you that. She kept telling you she couldn't say, making it seem like she didn't know. But she does know, she just chose not to tell you." I watched his face contort as he tried to control his frustration. "Plus, Annette was here Monday. She was at Fiona's last night and she's one of the ones who disappeared before your crew got to question everyone. Who goes on vacation on a Wednesday? It may be nothing, but you have to admit it's weird."

"I don't have to admit anything. Stop snooping around." He stomped down the hall without offering Declan or Mitzi a goodbye.

Declan took a coffee order from the guys and asked them to meet us at my shop. Wyatt was not an early riser and Nick had the worst sleeping schedule I had ever heard of. We knew at least the two of them hadn't ventured out of the hotel yet.

As usual, the coffee shop was the busiest place in town. We barely got to say 'hello' to Fiona, but she assured us she was fine from the previous evening. Declan leaned against the wall with his arms crossed while we waited for our coffee and I could see him trying not to smile.

"What are you not laughing at?"

He grinned at me. "So far this morning, another person assumed we're a couple, Mitzi referred to my cat as my bald spot, Alex suggested that same woman, who is old enough to be my grandmother, take a cold shower because of my presence, and he called me by my cat's name. One thing I will say, there is never a dull moment when you're around."

"I'm glad I can keep you entertained. On a serious note, though, did you notice the difference between the answers Detective Landry got and the ones we got? And why did she backtrack to tell us Annette was going to see family. I felt like she forgot to say it originally but needed us to know Annette had left town."

"I didn't realize it at the time, even though you hit me, but now that you say it, it is odd. Do you know anyone else who works at the town hall that we might be able to ask about Annette?"

"I don't, but in a town this size, she might be the only one." We gathered our trays of coffee and walked across the street. Nick, Wyatt, Falcon, and Clyde were all standing outside the door waiting for us. Once we were inside, Declan passed out the coffee and took my laptop while I sat down with my tablet to work on my client's drawing.

I thought I was going to have trouble concentrating but once I started, I fell into that familiar state of bliss that I get whenever I'm working on a project. For the next hour, I forgot everything that was bothering me. It didn't take as long as I thought it would to finish it. The image had been floating around in my mind for weeks, I just needed to get it in physical form so my client could see what I saw. Satisfied with what I accomplished, I turned my attention to my friends.

I cringed at the scene in front of me. Papers lay scattered around the floor, Wyatt and Falcon were using my tattoo chair as a footrest. Nick used one of my tables to hold his coffee cup, which was now without a lid and painted with streaks of coffee which had no doubt left a ring on the surface. Falcon had his shoes removed and perched himself on one of my chairs, his socked feet on the seat and his butt balanced on the back rest. As much as it pained me to see, I could hardly be mad since they were all there to help me.

"I certainly hope you're all planning to help me scour this place before we leave."

"We will." Falcon jumped down from the chair and looked around the room, his cheeks growing a faint pink. "Sorry about all this. I think we all kind of forgot where we are."

"That's okay. Did any of you find anything useful?"

"Yeah. I think we need to go talk to Maggie's boyfriend again." Wyatt gathered up three pages of her blog and walked them over to me. "I think it's a well-known fact that husbands, boyfriends, and partners are usually the main suspect in any murder. I looked it up online and it says strangulation is usually personal. Declan told us that Maggie's boyfriend was also seeing her best friend who happened to be the second victim, just luckier than Maggie. I don't know exactly what the motive might be, but Maggie knew he was seeing someone else. I'm just not sure she knew who.

"In the first article, she mentioned that she had a boyfriend and talks about how happy she is with him. Two months later, she says he's been acting differently, avoiding her, canceling plans. And then in the third one, her tone completely changes and she hints at knowing he's seeing someone else; she just doesn't have enough proof."

"I'm not sure I even understand how it's possible to do this in such a small town. Someone must have seen Carly and Caleb together at some point."

"Maybe. But they may not have known. I looked up a few pictures from their swim team." He turned his phone toward me. "There are a number of pictures of the two of them together. From the back, or from a distance, these girls would be hard to tell apart."

I took the phone from him and scrolled though the gallery. He was right. They were the same height, had the same build, wore their hair the same way. They looked exactly alike. "Caleb certainly has a type."

Something was bothering me; I just couldn't put my finger on it.

My appointment with my client went well but the whole time I felt like I was being watched. Declan made himself comfortable in the corner of my shop and I could feel him looking over at me every two minutes. I had to remind him several times that he was making me nervous.

While I was cleaning up the shop, I heard a sharp rapping sound on the door. It was dark outside, almost midnight, and the streetlights didn't offer much light in the doorway. Declan refused to let me answer it, so I kept cleaning. He came into the back room with Fiona by his side.

"Hey."

"I'm so happy you're still here. I wanted to tell you in person. Leyland turned himself in." She was so happy; her eyes were glistening.

"What?" *Leyland?*

"Yup. Earlier this evening. He's been at the station ever since. I'm not sure I believe it was him but who would say they're guilty if they're not?"

I raised my hand to my mouth in awe. I didn't know what to say.

"Anyway, I know it's late. I just wanted to let you know so you can sleep a little easier tonight."

"I appreciate you stopping by. Thank you."

Declan walked her out and came back over to hug me. "It looks like we have a reason to celebrate."

Chapter 18

Declan met me at the tattoo shop fifteen minutes before I expected my client to arrive. "The guys found a taco restaurant they want to hit up for dinner. I'm going to meet them over there if you're okay being by yourself?"

"Like I would ever deny you the chance to get tacos." The look in his eyes held concern and if I knew him as well as I thought I did, part of him wanted me to ask him to stay. I couldn't, even if I wanted to. I wouldn't keep him away from his friends and I certainly wouldn't stop him from trying a new taco joint.

"I'll only be about two hours. I'll come back here as soon as we're done."

"I'll be fine. I promise."

I sat at the counter making last minute changes to my client's drawing. I always found myself working until the client walked through the door. At exactly six o'clock, the front door opened and Andrew walked in. "Oh, hi. I didn't expect to see you."

"Yeah, I made the appointment under my real first name."

"I thought Andrew was your first name? Either way, go ahead and fill out this consent form. I'll just need to see your ID when you're done."

Having a job where you look at IDs from people every day showed how many people didn't use their given name in their daily lives. It was no wonder it was so easy for people to have multiple identities on the internet when they did it in real life, too.

"So, as we discussed via email, your tattoo is elaborate. The goal for tonight will be to get the outline done. After that, if there's time and you're still feeling all right, we can try to get all the shading done since there isn't much of it. Sound good?"

"Sounds great. I'm excited to see what you came up with."

"This is what I have drawn for you. Please look it over carefully. Make sure you like everything. If you want any changes, now's the time to tell me. Once the ink goes in, I can't change it." Being a tattoo artist for over ten years, I still couldn't believe how many clients would come in and request a change after a tattoo was complete with no understanding that the tattoo was permanent. I was impressed by how thoroughly Andrew looked the drawing over.

"This is perfect. Of course, it's hard to tell exactly what it'll look like once it's complete, but everything is right where I asked for it to be."

"Perfect. Give me just a minute to get the stencil and we'll get started." This was the first time I had been able to fully relax in over a week, not having anything to worry about. While I always valued my personal time, I realized this afternoon how much I took it for granted instead of being grateful for the mostly carefree life I was able to live. "Okay. Stand up straight, put your shoulders back, and breathe normally."

Everyone had that one task, whether it was at work or part of a hobby, they dreaded doing no matter how easy it was or how little time it took to accomplish. Putting stencils on was that task for me. I applied thousands of them over the years and I still loathed the idea of it. The last thing I ever wanted to do was have to apply it more than once. It was an easy task and took no more than two minutes, but I would choose to do a freehand tattoo any chance I got. With three different stencil parts, I was fortunate tonight and all three applied flawlessly the first time.

His email inquiry stated he was looking for an American traditional style with a twist. The twist being over-exaggerated traditional elements. The design took up the entire top of his back and went down to the middle. He requested a large ship with a skull and an eagle on two of the sails and an anchor, almost as large, with a pin-up sitting on it. During our email exchange, I tried to talk him into creating two separate tattoos, but he was set on having one design. This was one of those cases, because I opposed the idea, where I tried my best but ended up going with what the client wanted. Sometimes they listened and took my advice, other times they were set on an idea and I had to give in to make them happy.

"Okay. Go ahead and check it out in the mirror over there. Make sure you like the placement."

We spent the first thirty minutes discussing the town events that were coming up in the next few months. Fiona was right about it being an extremely social town.

According to Andrew, they had festivals, barbecues, and fairs that were all town sponsored plus all the cookouts residents hosted at their own houses.

"So, are you feeling better, safer, now that Leyland turned himself in?"

I should have expected the question or at least some conversation around the subject but I was trying to avoid it. It was a situation that I hadn't been able to escape for a week and I wanted to put it behind me. "I'm not sure how I feel to be honest. I should feel better because that means everyone will know it wasn't me." It was funny for me to think that was a selfish way to feel. "Something about the whole thing just doesn't seem right to me. I'm having a hard time believing Leyland can be guilty of murder."

He looked up at me from the corner of his eye. "Oh, does he not seem like a murderer to you?" The tone of his voice changed but I couldn't place the emotion.

Before I could answer, a bang sounded on the front window and I jumped. It sounded like someone threw a heavy object at it. I stood slowly, just enough so I could see over the counter. My heart skipped a beat when I saw Diesel's face peering in. "What in the world?" We left him at my house with Harley. *How did he get out?* I could see something sticking out of his mouth and I assumed he brought it over as a present. He did love giving gifts. I opened the front door and he bolted through before I had a chance to stop him. "Diesel. You know you're not allowed in here." I was working in the back room earlier and neglected to close the door when I came out. He zigzagged through the shop and ran into the back, jumping from the floor to the desk, and on to the highest shelf I had, the only one

I couldn't reach even with a ladder. I could still see the item in his mouth but no amount of convincing or putting my hand toward him would make him drop it. I didn't want him in the shop for sanitary reasons, but I didn't think he was coming down any time soon. Maybe he was lonely. I knew Harley wasn't the most lovable or friendly companion.

I went back to the front room and Andrew was still lying on the table, right where I had left him. He didn't seem disturbed by the disruption at all. "I am so sorry about that. I don't know what's gotten into him." I pulled on a fresh pair of gloves and picked up my machine. "Anyway... I don't know what a murderer should seem or look like. You hear all the time on documentaries and on the news that people never would have guessed that a certain individual could be capable of such acts. Then, other times, you can meet someone and you immediately know they probably have bodies hidden in their basement. I guess one never knows for sure." At my last comment, Andrew tensed and slid across the table so he could turn over. I was glad I didn't have a needle anywhere near him.

The look in his eyes was cold, his jaw muscles tense. "What would make you say that about bodies in the basement?"

I didn't understand why he got so mad about that comment. "It's just an off the wall comment that I would make about someone I got weird vibes from. Sometimes I might mean it but mostly it's just to add a bit of humor to what I'm saying." I stared at him for a moment, trying to piece everything together. Bits and pieces of information were floating around in my head, but nothing seemed to fit together.

He sat up and swung his legs over the side of the table. "I thought, when Leyland turned himself in, you would be smart enough to leave your little sleuthing ways behind, but apparently, you don't know when to quit." His entire face turned a shade of magenta I had never seen on a human and now I could place the anger in his voice.

Heat rose to my own face and my stomach tied in a knot. This wasn't how I expected the evening to go. "I don't understand what you're talking about. I haven't spoken to anyone since I found out about Leyland. Just because I didn't think he was capable doesn't mean he's not."

"Oh, so you just expect me to believe you made up line about the basement? It doesn't have anything to do with you snooping around people's houses?"

I narrowed my eyes, trying to process where our conversation was going. "I never snooped around people's homes. I went to their homes and knocked on their doors just like I did with you."

"Well then. I guess we're going to do this the hard way. I have to tell you, I'm a little disappointed because I actually kind of like you."

"What are you talking about?" I tried to roll my chair back without him noticing but he wrapped his feet around the cylinder.

"We're not going to do that." He shook his head. "Sally Jo told me she thought you were going to be a problem."

I never got her name while we were at the town hall, but I knew it had to be her. "You have Annette, don't you? Did you kill her?"

"Not yet. She needs to transfer money to me first. Money that should be mine."

"You're the other relative of Maggie's; the one people didn't know about."

He reached into his pocket and pulled out a strap. Probably the same one he used to kill Maggie and hurt Carly. "That's exactly the problem. I'm always the one people don't know about, the one people forgot about, the one no one cares about. I'm sick of it. It may not make anyone recognize me or accept me, but I want what's rightfully mine."

I had no idea how much time had passed but I wanted to keep him talking. I had no way to reach my phone and I wanted to give Declan plenty of time to get back. I just hoped he didn't decide to stay out longer or make any extra stops on his way back to the shop. "We read the blog we found at your house, the one where Maggie said that someone she knew was going to steal money. That was about you, wasn't it?"

Sweat was starting to drip from his temples. "It was, but I'm not stealing it and I didn't know about the article until after she died."

My eyes darted from side to side. There was nowhere for me to go from the position we were both in. I was getting answers, but I knew it was only a matter of time before he jumped at me and tried to strangle me, too. "How were you related to her?"

"She's my niece. But, just like her aunt and her father, she didn't want anything to do with me. The only reason she even talked to me was because I was her coach."

"You didn't get along with any of your family?" My heart was pounding and my skin was hot. I was running out of questions, which also meant I was running out of time.

He wrapped the strap around his hand and then unwound it, over and over. I took it as a sign of agitation. "I never did. Annette and Maggie's father were brother and sister. Full blood, you know, real family? They never accepted me as being one of them, no matter how hard I tried, because our parents adopted me."

"Where are Maggie's parents?"

"Gone. Her mother left soon after she was born, just gave her up and walked away. Her father died when she was three."

"Who raised her?"

"My parents, until she was eighteen. Then they kicked her out."

"Why did you kill her?" There was no point in delaying any longer. I wanted to know the truth.

"I thought it was Carly." He lowered his head just enough to tell me he was telling the truth.

My jaw dropped. "You didn't mean to hurt Maggie. You were going after Carly and you mistook Maggie for her? What did Carly have to do with any of it?"

"I never would have hurt Maggie. Despite how she treated me, I loved her. Carly, on the other hand, is cold and uncaring. She tried to blackmail me to give her the top spot on the team. She overheard a conversation between me and Sally Jo and got it all on video. We were talking about kidnapping Annette and making her transfer half the money she inherited because that should have been mine. But kids and their phones these days. They have proof of everything."

"And you saw Carly and Annette talking at Fiona's barbecue the other night. Did she tell her?"

"No. But I couldn't risk it any longer."

"That makes sense." It didn't make any sense. There was no reason for Carly to say anything if Maggie was already dead. She would have gotten the spot she wanted. "Why me? I didn't even know you. Why did you try to frame me for her murder?"

He laughed harder than was necessary. "Convenience. You were the new person in town. An easy target, especially since Annette had been running her mouth, trying to poison your name. The argument between you and Maggie was a bonus, pure gold in my eyes."

That was probably the furthest he thought his plan through. "I'm curious, though, what are you going to do if Annette refuses to transfer any money to you? I mean, you can't really kill her because then you would lose all chances of getting any of it. You'd be alone; left with no sister, a dead niece, and no inheritance." I heard Diesel jump from the shelf to the desk. The noise was soft but there was no mistaking the sound of his paws.

"You know what, Dakota? I think I'm done answering your questions." He kicked my chair back hard enough that I lost my balance and fell to the side. He loomed over me with the strap pulled between his hands.

I put my hands up to try to slow him down. "Wait. They think Leyland is guilty. You don't have to do this. If you kill me, they'll know it wasn't him. They'll continue to investigate."

"I'll take the risk."

He lunged at me and I rolled to the side, pushing the chair at him. I scrambled to get to my feet, but he grabbed my ankle and pulled me back down. His knee dug into my upper back; I couldn't breathe. I trapped one of my arms beneath me when I fell, but raised the other above my head so he couldn't get to my neck. I felt as though time had completely stopped. I could feel the beat of the music but couldn't make out any of the words. I saw a flash of movement beside me and heard Andrew cry out. *Diesel.* I took the opportunity and used all the strength I had to push myself up as hard as I could. The back of my head slammed into him and from the force of the impact, I guessed I had hit his face.

Stumbling first, I found my footing and ran toward the back room, forgetting my desk was still the only thing holding the back door closed. The full weight of Andrew's body slammed against me and I fell to the floor, cracking my head against the cement. In the distance, I heard someone call out my name before everything went black.

Chapter 19

I couldn't open my eyes, but I could hear someone calling my name repeatedly. I heard Diesel meow and felt his sticky tongue, like Velcro, caress the tip of my nose.

"Dakota. Wake up." *Declan.*

I pulled myself to a sitting position the best I could and flinched when I touched the side of my head. "Declan?" Diesel curled up in my lap and mewled.

"Hey. Alex just got here. Are you okay?" He knelt beside me and rested his hands on my shoulders.

"I think so. Did you get Andrew?"

He nodded. "We did. Falcon and I rode back here together after dinner. It's a good thing we got here when we did."

I tried to smile but every part of my face hurt. "I tried to keep him talking as long as I could. He killed Maggie."

"We know."

There was something else I needed to tell him, but my head was foggy. "He told me something..." It was right there; I was having trouble placing it. *His house. Money. The town hall.* "Annette." I practically screamed her name. "She's at his house. He kidnapped her." I struggled, trying to get to my feet, but crashed back to the floor.

"You stay here. I'll go check on her."

He yelled toward Alex on his way through the shop. "Annette is at Andrew's house. We're going to get her. Get Dakota medical attention *now*."

The next time I opened my eyes, a sharp pain sliced through them and tore into my brain. The lights were so bright. I cringed and crushed them shut again, moaning.

"Dakota? Are you awake?" Declan gathered my hand in his and sat on the side of the bed. "How are you feeling?"

My head throbbed with every word he spoke. "It hurts."

"I know it does. They had to take you to the hospital to evaluate your injuries. You're going to be okay after some rest."

"It doesn't feel like it. Why are the lights so bright?" I pulled my hand up to shield my face before trying to open my eyes again. "Ow."

"We can turn them off. Your face is swollen a lot, especially around your eye. But it could have been so much worse."

I sighed. "I may agree with you once the throbbing in my brain goes away. I feel like I'm going to be sick."

"It'll go away."

"Is it bad? My face, I mean?" I watched him squint.

"It's... not the best I've ever seen you look. Just bruises and swelling, nothing permanent." His lips shifted into his crooked smile. "That bandage on your head, though? It makes you look like the karate kid."

"Should I thank you for coming to my rescue, Mr. Miyagi?"

"I think you should. But before that, Alex is here. He has a couple questions for you if you're feeling up to answering them."

I was not up to answering them. I didn't want anything to do with Alex right now. All I wanted to do was go back to sleep. I knew it would be futile to deny him the time because if I did, he would still be here, waiting, after I napped. I nodded and immediately regretted it. With the lights off, it was much more tolerable to keep my eyes open and look around the room. I found him leaning against the wall in his classic stance with his arms crossed over his chest. "Go ahead."

Declan spent the next three days at my house, making sure I was okay. I had to reschedule four clients, which I never do, but I needed time for the swelling around my eye to go away. I needed to be able to see to give my clients the quality they expected from my tattoos.

Declan and Falcon found Annette tied to a chair in Andrew's basement and found Sally Jo curled up on the closet floor in the spare bedroom. Just as Andrew had spewed his entire story to me, Sally Jo did the same to Alex. She told him everything she knew about Andrew, Annette, and the role Carly played in everything by threatening to expose his secret. It seemed to everyone who knew them that Carly and

Maggie were the worst best friends ever. After everything that happened, it was obvious why they were so close. It was because neither of them cared about another human being.

I took one full day to rest and then Declan and I spent the next two days walking around the town green and sitting by the fountain. I didn't want to stay cooped up inside all day. Annette saw us a few times while we were around town and politely nodded Declan's way. She never thanked him for coming to her rescue or apologized for how she perceived him but her general attitude toward him had changed. It wasn't the perfect scenario, but I didn't expect much more from Annette.

Alex stopped by my house once to see how I was feeling and to let us know the court denied Andrew bail. Like Annette, he never apologized for accusing me of being a murderer, but his tone and demeanor were different. It felt like he had a respect for me that he didn't have before. I asked him about Leyland and why he turned himself in even though he wasn't guilty, but he never got a straight answer from him. I assumed it was guilt for not knowing who Maggie truly was.

It was a little late, but I did have to order a new back door for my shop and Declan helped me install the deadbolt before he told me he had to go back home. Of everything that happened over the last two weeks, that felt like the worst. I enjoyed having him and Diesel around, but there was something else, a feeling that I couldn't quite place.

Monday morning, exactly two weeks after these events began, I walked Declan out to my driveway. "I really can never thank you enough for everything you've done for me." I looked deep into his eyes. "Really, thank you."

"I hope you didn't think I would let you go through that by yourself."

I set Diesel in his basket and said goodbye to him before turning back to Declan. "I'm going to miss you."

He rested his hands on both sides of my face and leaned forward, gently kissing my forehead. "There is never a dull moment when you're around, Dakota." He pulled his helmet over his head and drove off.

My eyes filled with tears at both relief from the weight of the previous weeks and the knowledge of not knowing how soon I would see him again.

Do you want to keep reading? Continue on for a sample of *Calculated in Color*, book 2 of the Dakota Maddison Tattoo Shop Mystery series.

Calculated
In
Color

A Dakota Maddison
Tattoo Shop Mystery
Book 2

Chapter 1

I stayed up way too late enjoying the barbecue and bonfire with my friends. I hadn't seen any of them, except Falcon, since the week of my grand opening. This coming weekend is the fourth of July and all the guys came out to celebrate the holiday with me. Last time they were all here, I was under suspicion of murder and all my attention was focused on that and the shop's opening going smoothly. I'm looking forward to being able to spend quality time with them over the next few days.

I have one tattoo appointment scheduled for later this afternoon. Because the shop has been closed for the last two days, I'm going in early to give it a thorough cleaning. Every time I close for more than a day, I find it necessary to scour every surface, the doorknobs, chairs, floor, counters, to ensure the sanitary conditions.

I put my windows down to enjoy the breeze on my drive over. The sun already sat high and the air hung thick with humidity. After four months, it still brought me great joy driving over and seeing my shop, knowing how much effort I put into it. All traces of the spray paint someone used to brand me a murderer, just a few months ago, were gone and from the outside, it looked professional and welcoming. I sighed looking at the camera mounted to the outside. I put it up for safety when I first arrived in town, but it felt out of place now.

I dropped my keys and bag on the counter and started toward the back of the shop to turn the lights on. Despite being late morning, the shop remained dark without help from artificial lights. My foot connected with something on the floor, sending it rolling away. I stopped and looked down. Bottles of ink were scattered across the floor, the organizer that had previously been fastened to the wall, now lay in pieces; shards of the thick plastic had been flung in all directions.

"What the..." I stepped over a few bottles, still wanting the light so I could see what happened. Right before walking into the back room, I froze. A body lay motionless in the doorway, their head pointing toward me. "Not again." I pulled my phone from my pocket and turned on the flashlight. It gleamed off a large knife protruded from the victim's back and a puddle of what appeared to be blue and purple ink and blood mixed in a nauseating form reminiscent of a painter's pallet on the floor.

So much for enjoying the festivities and quality time with my friends.

Author's Note

When you are finished reading, if you do not keep physical books, please consider donating your copy to your local library for their book sale or to your local prison book program.

Author's Bio

Trish recently moved across the country where she found her forever home, enjoying the desert sunshine and wildlife all year long. She was born and raised in a small town in northern Connecticut. Growing up, she was always fascinated by unsolved mysteries and true crimes as well as the psychological elements behind them. As an avid reader, her go to books are thriller/suspense, true crime, and cozy mysteries.